He started to step out the door but stopped, gazing at her with eyes that told her their kiss had been special to him, too. "One for the road?"

Feeling more feminine than she had in a long time, Sammy gave him a demure smile then stood on tiptoe and kissed his cheek.

"Nice, but not exactly what I had in mind." Wrapping his arms about her again, his lips sought hers, and his kiss made her head spin. "Good night. Thanks for a great evening."

Dipping her head to avoid his gaze, Sammy backed away, her legs trembling and threatening to crumple beneath her. "Good night, Ted."

After gazing at her for a few more seconds, he stepped outside, closing the door behind him. Sammy turned and leaned against it, her fingers gently touching her lips, as if by touching them she could preserve the kisses he'd bestowed upon them.

Her moment of overwhelming joy collapsed as her hand went to her heart. *I have to tell him. Soon. Our attraction for each other may never go beyond where it is now, but it's not fair to keep something like this from him. It seems that, just by being my friend, he has the right to know the heart beating within me is not my own.*

JOYCE LIVINGSTON loves to write and feels writing inspirational romance is her God-given ministry. A wife, mother, grandmother, and former television broadcaster, she has many life experiences from which to draw. Her books have won numerous awards, including Heartsong's Contemporary Author of the Year in 2003 and 2004, and Book of the Year numerous times. She has well over twenty books in print, and more contracted and in the writing stage.

Books by Joyce Livingston

HEARTSONG PRESENTS

Don't miss out on any of our super romances. Write to us at the following address for information on our newest releases and club information.

Heartsong Presents Readers' Service
PO Box 721
Uhrichsville, OH 44683

Or visit www.heartsongpresents.com

Secondhand Heart

Joyce Livingston

Heartsong Presents

In addition to my beloved deceased husband, Don Livingston, to whom I dedicate every book I write, I want to dedicate this book to a very special woman—my oldest daughter, Dawn Lee Johnson. May God add his blessings to her life and give her the desires of her heart. I love you, Dawn Lee.

A note from the Author:
I love to hear from my readers! You may correspond with me by writing:

Joyce Livingston
Author Relations
PO Box 721
Uhrichsville, OH 44683

ISBN 1-59789-135-5

SECONDHAND HEART

All scripture quotations are taken from the King James Version of the Bible.

All of the characters and events in this book are fictitious. Any resemblance to actual persons, living or dead, or to actual events is purely coincidental.

Our mission is to publish and distribute inspirational products offering exceptional value and biblical encouragement to the masses.

PRINTED IN THE U.S.A.

handed one to Sammy then shook her head. "Sweetie, aren't you being a little too self-conscious? You waited for nearly two years for that heart, and you certainly aren't the first young woman to have a heart transplant. Others out there are just like you."

Sammy stared into the cup. "I'm sure you're right. I remember how frightened I was the first time I heard that word—transplant. To think a doctor could actually insert someone else's heart into another human being was mind-boggling, and I never thought it would happen to me." She sniffed at the coffee's delicious aroma then blew to cool it. "Face it, Mom. What man is going to want a woman who has an ugly scar like this and a life expectancy of ten years, maybe less? Most men want children. Maybe a guy could get past the medication I have to take and seeing this ugly scar every day of his life. But what man would want to live with the idea of losing his wife, knowing unless he remarried, he'd probably have to raise his children alone? Certainly no man I know."

Mrs. Samuel slipped her arm around her daughter's shoulders and gave her a hug. "You may not know a man like that now, but if God wants you to marry, He's probably already preparing some man's heart to accept you the way you are."

Sammy looked toward her apartment's small living room where the TV blared out her nephew and nieces' favorite cartoon. "But what about these precious children, Mom? Even if a man could circumvent the heart thing, what about them? They're a part of me, at least until their mother comes back for them. Any man who would accept me would also have to accept these children who are living with me."

"Oh, honey, have faith. God will give you the understanding

and strength you need. In the meantime, we have to pray your sister will wake up, realize what she is missing, and come back for them."

"I feel so inadequate. Other than the books I read, I know practically nothing about parenting. I may be feeling my way along as I go, but I'm doing the best I can. Honest I am."

"You're doing a wonderful job. You have more patience with those children than I had with you and your sister."

Sammy gazed at her silver-haired mother. Though the events of the past few years had aged her, to Sammy she was still beautiful. "I'm glad she left them with me instead of expecting you and Dad to care for them. With his poor health and your having to work to make up for the loss of his income, the two of you could never have taken them in. And I couldn't have made it these last few months since my surgery if you and Daddy hadn't offered to come to Denver and stay with me."

Her mother settled back in the chair with a sigh, folding her hands in her lap. "I wish we could have done more."

"You've already done more than you should. It breaks my heart to think Tawanda would desert Simon, Tina, and Harley as she did, especially since she was aware of my heart problem. But I'm sure she knew you and Dad would jump in and help me."

Tears misted over her mother's eyes. "I thought for sure she'd only be gone a couple of weeks and then come back."

"I can't imagine a woman leaving her children for any reason, especially some motorcycle-riding, tobacco-chewing, jobless guy, just because he paid her a little attention."

"I don't know where your father and I went wrong with your sister."

Sammy gave her mother's shoulder an appreciative squeeze. "You and Dad were the best parents ever. It was Tawanda who went wrong."

"Even though they drive your father crazy and his nerves are frazzled, we've enjoyed being here with you and our grandchildren. His declining health has really taken its toll. I've worried about him. He seems to be getting weaker every day. I'm afraid it's time to take him home."

"I know, and it makes me cry to see him this way. He's always been so strong. I'm sure the six of us being cramped up in my tiny apartment hasn't helped." Sammy gestured toward a photo magnet on her refrigerator. "Sad, isn't it? I doubt little Harley would remember her mom if she walked in that front door. What kind of mother would name her sweet baby girl after her boyfriend's motorcycle?"

Mrs. Samuel shook her head. "At least she didn't choose Gold Wing as her middle name. I love Tawanda as much as I love you, but her actions and her uncaring attitude break my heart. Only the Lord can bring her to her senses. We just have to keep praying for her."

Sammy nodded, well remembering the day her sister left and the trauma it had brought. "I pray for her constantly, Mom. I love these children, and I know they love me, but like most kids, they want their mom. I enjoy having them here and would be happy to keep them always, but they're *her* children. It'd be just like Tawanda to turn up unannounced on my doorstep, ready to waltz right back into their lives, expecting them to go with her as if nothing ever happened. As much as I'd like to see her little family reunited, I couldn't stand the idea of seeing them uprooted and hurt again."

"Then there's the other side of the coin, Sammy. What if Tawanda never comes back after them? Are you prepared to care for them until they're old enough to be out on their own? Honey, I think you need to face the fact that your sister was never cut out for motherhood. I hate to say it, but I suspect each of those darlings was the product of an evening of nothing more than lust and carelessness."

Sammy let out a deep sigh. "I've thought that, too. I feel sorry for my sister and try to keep her memory alive by talking about her and showing her pictures to the children so they'll remember her, but how can I explain her absence to them? The lack of phone calls and letters? She has no idea how much she's giving up by not being with these amazing children."

"They're amazing because of you, Sammy, and the love and care you've given them since she left. Good thing you thought to get her to sign temporary custody over to you so you'd have the power to take care of any emergencies that came up." Mrs. Samuel took Sammy's hand and gave it a gentle squeeze. "When your heart doctor gives you your final release, sweetie, why don't you come back to Nashville to live? We have excellent doctors there. I know you're happy living here in Denver and you like your job, but you're still recuperating and will be for a while. You need help. I'd like to stay in Denver and continue to care for you and the children, but your father needs to be back in his own home and near his doctors. And I can't expect my boss to hold my job much longer."

Sammy drank the last of her coffee, making a face when she realized it had turned cold. "Your offer is tempting."

"It's going to be some time before you'll be operating at full speed. If you come back to Nashville, I can continue to help you and the children until you're able to take on a new job. There's plenty of room in that big old house for all of us. You and the kids can have the entire second floor. Moving back would be better for everyone."

Sammy sent another glance toward the living room. "But if I quit my job here, how will I support myself and the children? Their mother hasn't sent a penny since she's been gone. If Uncle Mort hadn't put Tawanda's and my names on that insurance policy, I don't know what I would have done, but that money isn't going to last forever."

Mrs. Samuel rose and filled their cups. "Well, getting a job in Nashville shouldn't be too difficult for you, not with your exemplary employment record. Dozens of companies could use a good customer service director. With your experience and the kind of references your boss would give you, I'm sure you'll have no trouble finding a job when you're ready to take one on. Meantime, your dad and I can help with finances. I've been saving what Mort left me for a rainy day. I can't think of a better way to spend that money."

Sammy thoughtfully twisted a lock of hair around her finger. "It would be nice to live closer to you and Dad and to get back to my home church."

Mrs. Samuel smiled at her daughter. "Then it's settled. Your father and I will go home this week. But as soon as the doctor gives you the okay, I'll fly back to help you pack up, and we'll all head for Nashville. Agreed?"

Sammy pondered her question before answering. Moving back to Nashville would be the best solution for everyone, but did she really want to move back? Give up her apartment, the Denver church where she worshipped, and the job she loved and had worked so hard to get?

Raising her brow in question, her mother gave her a gentle nudge. "Say yes, dear. It's the best answer for everyone."

A job and an apartment are just things, Sammy reasoned as she considered her options. *Being with those you love is what's important. And even though I love my church here in Denver, I love my home church in Nashville even more. Once the children get used to it, they'll love it, too.* "You're right, Mom. Moving back is the best answer. With all that's happening in our lives now, the children and I need to be nearer you and Dad. God has given me the awesome privilege and responsibility of taking care of Simon, Tina, and Harley by making sure they are loved and have a solid Christian upbringing. It's my mission in life, my God-appointed mission."

A sudden peace came over her as she lifted her face and gazed into her mother's eyes. "But if I go, you have to promise not to baby me like I'm an invalid, and I don't want to have to discuss my operation or my new heart with anyone. The less said about it, the better. I want to get over this thing as soon as possible and get on with my life, whatever may be left of it. I don't want anyone feeling sorry for me."

Her mother smiled and raised her right hand. "I promise."

Sammy felt a slight tug on her shirt. "Well, hi, little sweetheart. Did you have a good nap?"

Tina grinned up at her. "Yes, Mommy."

Kneeling beside the child, Sammy wrapped an arm about her tiny waist. "You mustn't call me Mommy, sweetie. I'm your aunt." She bobbed her head toward the shelf above the gas fireplace. "Mom, would you please hand me Tawanda's picture?"

Once she had the photograph in hand, she pointed to the image of her sister's face. "See, that's your mommy. She's beautiful just like you."

Tina gave her a puzzled look. "But why can't I call you mommy? My friend Lacy calls the lady she lives with Mommy."

"That's because that lady *is* her mommy. Your mommy is away for a while, that's all—but she's still your mommy."

"Where is she? Why isn't she here with me the way Lacy's mommy is with her?"

The wide-eyed innocent look on Tina's face ripped at Sammy's heart. "I don't know exactly where she is at this moment, but we have to keep praying for her that God will bring her back to us, safely and as soon as possible."

Tina lowered her lip in a pout. "I want you to be my mommy."

"I'd like to be your mommy, but you already have a mommy. And you know what? You look very much like her."

Tina glanced at the picture. "But I don't want that mommy. She never comes to see me. I want you."

Sammy pulled the irresistible child onto her lap, lovingly brushing a curl from her forehead. "Please try to understand, precious. Mommy is busy right now. I have an idea. Why don't you draw a picture for her? Then, when she sends us her address, I'll mail it to her." She leaned toward the coffee table, picked up the tin of crayons she kept there for the children, and handed them to Tina. "Maybe when Harley wakes up, she'd like to draw a picture for your mother, too."

Tina showed little enthusiasm, but she took the crayons, scooted off Sammy's lap, and padded toward the bedroom.

Sammy's mother sat down beside her and took her hand,

giving it an affectionate squeeze. "I'd say you handled that just fine."

"I hope so, Mom. I want the children to think well of their mother, but it's hard when she never writes or calls them. I couldn't even give Tina a straight answer when she asked where her mother was."

"God knows where she is, sweetie. We have to give Tawanda over into His hands. She's out of our reach."

"I know, Mom. I know."

one

Three years later

Sammy spotted a couple of empty chairs next to the railing at the far end of the upper deck of Nashville's famous *General Jackson* riverboat. She made her way toward them and seated herself, closing her eyes and lifting her face to the sun. What a glorious day it was, and she had it all to herself. "Don't worry about anything, Sammy," her mother had told her when she'd arrived at her apartment that morning to care for the children. "They'll be fine. Just enjoy yourself. You deserve a break."

Sammy adjusted her sunglasses then smiled. *I don't know about deserving a break, but it is nice to have an entire day to myself.*

Her smile disappeared. She hadn't heard from her sister in nearly a year, and then it was only a postcard. For all she knew, Tawanda could have disappeared off the face of the earth. She wondered if the man she'd left with was treating her well. It seemed every man Tawanda had ever dated had been an abuser of some sort, by either taking everything he could get from her or tiring quickly of her company and shoving her around, blacking her eyes, or doing even worse.

Nearly four years since his mother disappeared, Simon still talked about some of those beatings. Cowering in the closet and frightened out of their wits, he and Tina had witnessed many of them, and those experiences had left emotional scars on them both, especially Simon. Being the oldest, he remembered things more vividly than Tina. Fortunately, since Harley had been a baby, Sammy was sure she wouldn't remember and have the emotional baggage to carry around the rest of her life as her siblings would.

"This seat taken?"

Startled by the voice, she sat up straight and opened her eyes, shielding them from the morning sun, which made her intruder nothing more than a dark profile against its glare. "No, I don't think so." She'd hoped no one would decide to sit in that chair. It would have been nice to be alone for a change. To someone whose life was filled with work, kids, doctor appointments, and church activities, the solitude had sounded inviting. "At least no one was sitting there when I came up here."

The man moved past her and placed his soft-drink cup on the small table between them before sitting down. "The music got a little loud down there." He gestured toward the stairs leading to the lower deck. "I enjoy music, but my ears can take only so much of it at those decibels."

"I know exactly what you mean. It was loud for me, too."

"Have you done this riverboat thing before?"

For the first time since he'd become a full-fledged person and not a silhouette against the sun, she looked up into his face. "No. Even though I've lived in Nashville most of my life, this is my first time." Glancing sideways while trying not to be too obvious, she sized him up. Tall, but not too tall. Nearly average build, but muscular enough to look as if he worked out. Well-coordinated shirt and trousers, better than most guys his age. Maybe his mom helped him pick out his clothes.

He pulled his sunglasses from his pocket and slipped them on. "First time for me, too."

Her next glance went to where she usually looked when meeting a man for the first time, though she didn't know why. Habit probably. No wedding ring, but that didn't mean anything. Some men never wore a ring, even if they were married. What difference did it make anyway? The guy was only looking for an empty chair. She leaned her head back against the tall deck chair and closed her eyes again.

"You like country western?"

So much for closing her eyes! She'd hoped shutting them would put an end to their conversation. "Music?"

He grinned, causing the indentation in his chin to show prominently. "Yeah, music. I like most of it, but the guys where I work play it constantly. I get a little tired of it, especially the songs where some gal is moaning because her boyfriend is two-timing her or vice versa. I like the more toe-tapping ones. What kind do you like?"

"I can't remember the title, but my favorite country song is the one about a truck driver out on the road, thinking about his family and how he loves his wife and children and wishes he were home with them. Not many songs like that." *What's the matter with me? I should have simply nodded and kept quiet. I didn't have to give him a full answer.*

A smile brightened his handsome face. "I know exactly the song you mean. It's one of my favorites, too." He picked up the plastic drink cup he'd brought with him to the upper deck. "Would you like a cold drink? Ah—I don't know your name, and I hate to call you 'hey-you.'"

Not sure she wanted to share such personal information

with a stranger, Sammy tugged her collar up closer about her neck and paused before answering. She decided it wouldn't hurt to let him know the nickname her parents and friends called her instead of Rosalinda, her real first name. She gave him a guarded smile. "My friends call me Sammy."

He stuck out his hand. "Hi, Sammy. I'm Ted. Now what will it be? Iced tea? Lemonade? What? I need to go after a refill anyway."

"Iced tea will be fine, thank you. Unsweetened."

His face contorted into a playful frown. "You're a Southerner, and you want unsweetened tea? Didn't your mama teach you better than that? I thought all Southern ladies drank sweet tea."

She shrugged. "Guess Mom failed in her duty. I've never liked sweet tea."

He rose and gave her a teasing wink. "Unsweetened it is. I'll be right back. Save my seat."

She watched as he crossed the deck and disappeared down the stairwell. Ted. What a nice old-fashioned name. She hadn't met anyone named Ted since Ted Maxwell sat behind her in the fourth grade. But, nice or not, she would have preferred spending the rest of the day alone. Oh, well. He'd leave after a while. Surely he hadn't come alone. His friends were probably on the lower deck. She'd barely settled back in her chair when he returned, carrying two glasses of tea.

"Unsweetened for you. Sweet for me. Can't help it. I'm a typical Southerner."

She thanked him then took a long sip of the cool drink. It tasted good. She hadn't realized she was so thirsty.

"Hope I didn't take your boyfriend's seat."

Sammy nearly choked. "I'm here alone."

He gaped at her. "Alone? Really? A pretty woman like you? That's hard to believe."

Embarrassed at having admitted such a personal thing, Sammy felt a flush rise to her cheeks. "Yes, really. Believe it or not, some people enjoy doing things alone."

He lifted his hands in surrender. "Sorry. I guess my question sounded a bit flippant. It's just that you're so—beautiful—well, I figured some lucky man had escorted you here. Actually"— he paused with a bashful grin—"I came alone, too."

As good-looking and well mannered as he was, Sammy found his statement hard to believe, too.

"Someone gave me two tickets. My buddy was supposed to come with me, but he had to cancel at the last minute. I almost didn't come but then decided, why not? I was off today and had nothing better to do, and I love being out on the river."

Without responding, after taking another sip of tea, Sammy leaned her head back again.

"Actually I was kinda glad for a chance to spend the day alone. I moved into my new apartment about six months ago and was enjoying it until I invited my older brother, his wife, and their kids to move in with me while he looks for a job. The company he worked for in Miami is downsizing, and he got the ax. The two weeks they originally said they'd be staying with me have turned into six weeks. I hate to say it, but those kids are driving me up the wall. I used to think I'd like to get married and have a houseful of them; now I'm not so sure."

Sammy wanted to speak up in defense of growing children and their sometimes loud, unruly exuberance for life but decided not to. The last thing she wanted was to get into a conversation about childrearing, which would inevitably lead to having to explain that her sister had abandoned her children. She simply nodded.

"I had no business saying those things about my nephews. The kids aren't to blame. My brother and his wife believe in permissiveness. You know, without discipline, ground rules, penalties for misbehavior, the whole enchilada."

Sammy nodded. "I think every child needs parameters. It gives them a feeling of security."

He wagged his head approvingly. "Like a lot of guys my age, I've filled my apartment with all sorts of electronic gadgets. The first thing I did after I offered to let them stay with me was to make space for all my computer stuff in my room and put a lock on my door. I figured that would save a lot of hassles. I even bought a used computer from a friend, set it up in the living room and let them have at it, which made them happy and kept me happy, too. Unfortunately, one of them wiped the hard drive clean the first day. But good ol' Uncle Ted reloaded everything, and they were back in business within minutes."

"Adding that used computer sounds like a great idea."

He nodded. "Yeah, it's worked out well and keeps them occupied. Don't get me wrong. I'm glad to help my brother out. . . . But enough about me." Smiling and tilting his head toward her, he lifted his brow. "Other than going on riverboat cruises alone, what else do you do for fun, Sammy?"

"Me? Work. Go to church. Teach a Sunday school class." She almost added she was the temporary custodian of three children but decided not to mention it.

"What's your job?"

She gave her mock turtleneck collar another tug. "I'm the customer service manager for a large national company."

"I'll bet you're good at it."

"I like to think so. How about you?"

"Fireman. At one of the smaller neighborhood fire stations. You know. On one day, off two. Today is one of my days off."

About to melt under the sun's rays, Sammy took off her jacket and draped it over the back of her chair. "It'd be nice to have two days off every third day like that. You like being a fireman?"

"Yep, wouldn't want to be anything else."

She could tell by his smile he meant it. "It's nice when people enjoy their jobs. I love my job, too, though I have to deal with many disgruntled people. Sounds crazy, but I actually enjoy working out their problems for them. It's a challenge."

"Do you ever have any customers who are simply impossible to work with?"

"I wish I could say no, but we're highly trained and know what to do, what not to do, and how to do what we can. That helps. After you've been there as long as I have, your reactions become second nature."

The loud speaker crackled, and then a heavy male voice announced, "The luncheon buffet is now being served on the main deck."

Ted rose and extended his hand. "Wanna humor a lonely guy and have lunch with him? I hate eating alone."

Sammy's grip tightened on her tea glass.

"Oh, come on. I'm harmless. Besides, there are a lot of people on board to protect you."

"Maybe it wouldn't—"

Lowering his hand, he backed away. "You don't have to explain. It's okay. I understand. You don't know me. If I were a woman I'd probably say no, too. It's been nice meeting you, Sammy. Enjoy the rest of your day." Spinning around on his heel, he moved in line with the others who were making their way down the stairs leading to the lower deck.

Sammy watched him go, wishing she'd accepted his invitation. Surprising herself, she leaped out of the chair and made her way to join him, breathlessly telling him, "If the invitation still stands, I'd love to have lunch with you."

Grinning, he motioned for her to step in front of him. "You bet it still stands. Thanks for changing your mind. You really deflated my ego. No one likes to be rejected."

"I wasn't rejecting you."

His grin widened. "I know. I'm just teasing, but I am glad you changed your mind."

They made their way through the abundant buffet line, taking small samples of nearly everything and laughing about the silly face the chef had carved into a watermelon, and then climbed the stairs to the upper deck.

"Ah, our seats are still there." Ted nodded toward the places they had temporarily vacated. "I guess when folks saw your jacket draped over the chair, they thought it'd been left there to save it."

Sammy's eyes widened. "I did leave my jacket. Where was my brain?"

He gave her a sheepish grin. "It was busy thinking up reasons you shouldn't have lunch with me."

She rolled her eyes. "No, it wasn't."

"Oh, yes, it was. Admit it."

"Okay, I'll admit, it did seem a bit awkward for me to have lunch with a man I'd just met. Satisfied?"

They enjoyed their lunch while discussing calories, carbohydrates, polyunsaturated fats, and other topics, laughing and talking like two old friends.

"Sit right there, and I'll go get us two big wedges of cheesecake." Ted stood. "Want strawberries or blueberries on yours?"

"Um, strawberries, but you don't have to get it for me."

"I want to get it for you. Not every day I have the privilege of serving such a lovely Southern lady."

"Even if she doesn't drink sweet tea?"

"Even then."

He was back in a flash as promised, with two large wedges of cheesecake topped with fresh strawberries. "One for you, madam, and one for me."

Sammy stared at the huge piece of cheesecake. "I could never eat that much cheesecake, even on an empty stomach. I'm already full. That's the biggest lunch I've eaten in a long time."

"Eat what you can. It really looks tasty."

Tasty? Wasn't that an old-fashioned term? Her father was the only man she knew who used that word to describe the foods he liked. She took the plate from his hand and sampled the delicious-looking concoction. "Oh, my. Just what I was afraid of. It's marvelous."

"I figured it would be. Now aren't you glad you tried it?"

Sammy licked at her lips. "Promise you'll stop me if I try to eat the whole thing?"

He raised his brow. "Me, stop you? No way. You're on your own. Me? I intend to eat every bite, every tiny morsel. This is a real treat. I'm used to cupcakes, cookies, and other things out of a package. Sara Lee and I get along real well in the kitchen. If it weren't for her frozen foods at the supermarket and the cooking the guys do at the fire station, I'd die of starvation."

Sammy ate until she could eat no more, then placed her fork on her plate. "I'm stuffed, Ted, and every bite of this fantastic lunch is going to show up on my hips." She realized it was the first time she'd called him by name. Did that mean she was finally comfortable with him? But as nice as he was, who wouldn't feel comfortable with him?

"But worth it, right?"

She rubbed at her tummy and let out a sigh. "Absolutely."

"We'll be getting off in an hour or so. Want to take a spin around the deck to walk off some of our lunch? I'd like to step out on the back of the lower deck and watch that big paddle wheel go around. This boat is amazing. Makes you think how different life must have been years ago when the river was filled with paddle wheelers."

Sammy had to admit she was tired of sitting in the same place so long, and what harm could a walk around the boat do? "Sure, a walk would be nice." After slinging her purse strap over her shoulder, she stood. "Lead the way."

The two strolled leisurely around the deck, talking about the intense growth of trees and the cabins along the shoreline, pausing now and then to watch a bird soar overhead. Eventually they walked down the staircase and out onto the lower deck, ending up leaning on the railing that separated them from the gigantic paddle wheel. They enjoyed the fine mist kicked up by its movement and listened to its rhythmic *swish, swish* as it rotated on its huge axis.

"I can't tell you how much I've enjoyed this day, Sammy," Ted shouted over the loud noise as the wheel whapped against the water. "I'm glad I didn't cancel when my buddy couldn't come."

"I've enjoyed it, too." And she had. More than she cared to admit. How long had it been since she'd carried on a conversation with a man, other than her father and a few male acquaintances at her church? It'd been nice talking with Ted. No commitments. No need to put on a façade. No reason to have to explain about her nieces and nephew being in her care. Thanks to him, it had been a lovely, refreshing day. One she would remember for a long time.

"We're pulling into the dock," the heavy male voice boomed out over the loud speakers. "For your safety, please remain on board until the boat is secured to its moorings and the gangway lowered. Thank you for spending the day with us on Nashville's famous *General Jackson*. We hope you've had a good time and will come and visit us again soon."

"Bummer. Looks like our boat ride is coming to an end." Ted cradled his hand about her elbow and nudged her toward the crowd assembling at the exit gate.

"Looks that way. I've really enjoyed it. It's been a great day."

"Ted! I didn't know you were on this boat."

The couple turned to take note of a man several yards behind them, waving and wearing a broad smile.

"Pete, hey—I didn't know you were on here either."

Letting go of her arm, Ted made his way back to the man whom Sammy assumed to be a close friend and gave his hand a hearty shake.

Grasping Ted's arm, the man tugged him toward several

other passengers. "I want you to meet my fiancée, Carla; my mother, Gladys; my dad, Robert—"

"Move along, folks," the crewman standing near the exit gate told the crowd in a friendly manner, motioning to the gangway. "For your safety and the safety of those near you, be sure to use the handrail."

The passengers around Sammy eased their way forward, moving her along with them. She glanced back at Ted. Finding him engaged in deep conversation with his friend's family, she stepped onto the gangway with the others and then onto the dock. When she turned and looked back at the departing crowd, Ted wasn't among them. He was still visiting with his friends, apparently oblivious to the fact that she wasn't still waiting for him and they hadn't said a proper good-bye. But what difference did it make? Why should he be concerned whether she'd waited or not? They'd never see each other again. They'd simply been two strangers who had spent a pleasant few hours together. That was all. But she had hoped he would leave his friends, catch up with her, and at least say good-bye.

Pushing aside her disappointment, she edged along the narrow dock and headed toward her car. Her day with Ted had been a good one, exactly what she'd needed to give her self-confidence a much-needed kick start. But the day was over, never to be repeated. She'd go her way and he'd go his, and life would move on.

Ted the fireman, one of the nicest men she'd ever met, would be just a pleasant memory.

two

Ted had hoped to see Sammy waiting for him when he excused himself and left his friend's family, but she was nowhere in sight. Most of the passengers had disembarked and were heading across the dock to the parking lot. *You're an idiot*, he told himself as he trudged down the gangway. *You spent most of the day with one of the nicest and prettiest women you've ever met, and you didn't even get her last name. Dumb. Dumb. Dumb.*

He'd nearly reached the landing when a thought occurred to him. Sammy had draped her jacket over a chair. Had she picked it up before they left the upper deck? He couldn't remember if she had. Turning quickly, just as the deckhand prepared to fasten the chain across the open section of the railing, he explained about her jacket, located the rear stairs, and hurried to the upper deck. Sure enough, there it was, exactly where she'd left it.

Now what? He had no address or phone number, no way to return it to her. As he lifted it from the chair, an idea struck him. Rushing back to the main deck, he thanked the deckhand, exited down the gangway, and headed toward the boat's ticket office.

"My friend left her jacket on the boat and will probably be calling about it." Picking up a pen that was lying on the counter, he wrote the word *Ted* and his phone number on a nearby scratch pad. "Her name is Sammy. Just tell her Ted has it and to give me a call, and I'll bring it by her apartment."

A slight frown creased the woman's brow. "You sure you don't want to leave it here? We have a lost-and-found box."

"Naw. It'll be a lot easier if I deliver it, rather than have her drive all the way back here."

"Why don't you just call her yourself?" She gestured toward the phone on the wall.

Clinging tightly to the jacket, he shook his head. "I doubt she's home yet. When she calls, just tell her I have her jacket." No way was he going to leave it behind. That jacket was his only link to Sammy.

After pulling a piece of transparent tape from its dispenser, the woman taped the information he'd given her on the wall next to the phone. "There you go. If she calls, I'll give her your message."

From time to time, Ted glanced at the jacket lying beside him in the front seat as he drove back to his apartment, grateful Sammy hadn't remembered to take it with her. When he reached home, he hung it carefully in his entry closet, smoothing out the sleeves to avoid wrinkles. It smelled pleasant. Like freshly cut flowers on a spring day. The fragrance hadn't overwhelmed him like the perfume of some of the women he'd dated, but he'd noticed it the moment he sat down beside her on the boat. It was one of the nicest fragrances he'd ever smelled. In fact, everything about her was nice.

There were no two ways about it.

He had to find Sammy, his mystery woman.

He should have gotten her last name.

He worked until dark, helping his brother change the

oil in his car then ran the washer and dryer, folding several loads of laundry. Next, since it was nearly impossible to avoid the endless array of questions from his nephews, he closed himself in his room, going through the stack of mail that had accumulated all week, doing anything he could to avoid thinking of Sammy.

Ted checked his phone at least once an hour to make sure it was working properly, but no call came from Sammy. Try as he may, though, even without her call, he couldn't get her off his mind. Something about that woman had drawn him to her the moment he'd sat down beside her on the paddle wheeler. Had it been her reserved attitude? Her reluctance to talk to a stranger?

Though he himself was shy by nature, his occupation as a fireman attracted women to him whether he showed any interest in them or not. Something about a man in uniform, whether military or civilian, seemed to have universal appeal to women. He grinned as he thought about it. Most of his single coworkers laughed about that well-known fact and bragged about how they'd used their uniform to its best advantage whenever they were around a woman they'd like to meet.

"We're their protectors," one of the guys on his shift had told him. "They trust us. We're the guys who come to their rescue when they're in need. If I'm in uniform and I see an attractive woman, all I have to do is give her a smile and she's mine."

With an exaggerated chuckle, Ted had poked his finger into the man's slightly pudgy stomach. "Even with that gut of yours?"

His coworker protruded his stomach out even further. "Yep, even with this, but when she gets a load of these biceps"—he paused long enough to strike a muscleman pose—"she forgets all about the gut."

Ted sobered. Unfortunately, what the man had said was true. He'd seen it too often. Women *did* gravitate to men in uniform, especially firemen, law-enforcement officers, and pilots. Spending twenty-four-hour shifts at the firehouse, he and his buddies had plenty of time for talking, and talk they did. Though he often figured much of what they said was nothing *but* talk, exaggerated to impress one another, some of it was probably true. A high percentage of the men he worked with had been divorced at least once, some several times.

Some of their conversations were a little on the shady side, but most were okay, and since he wanted to fit in, he participated with exuberance when he could. He could hold his own with the best of them when it came to sports, cars, motorcycles, world events, and other topics of general appeal, but not when it came to women. As far as he was concerned, that subject was taboo. He hated it when men bragged about their conquests and discussed things that were too personal even to mention. Times like that, he quietly slipped away and went to his bunk to read.

By the time Ted turned in at half past eleven, he still hadn't heard from Sammy.

Maybe he never would.

He had barely crawled into bed and switched off the light when he heard a crash from somewhere in his apartment. Jumping up, he rushed out into the living room to find the lamp from the credenza shattered into a million pieces. "What happened?" he asked his sister-in-law who was standing there in her robe with some sort of green goop on her face.

"Both Robbie and Billy were having trouble going to sleep, so I told them they could watch TV for a while," she explained, cuddling her eight- and ten-year-olds to her side. "I guess your lamp got bumped somehow."

Ted stared at her in disbelief. "Bumped? How? It was clear on the other side of the room."

"Billy was running around the room messing with the remote control, so I threw a pillow at him," Robbie explained, pointing at his brother. "I guess it hit your lamp."

Ted shook his head. "That lamp was inexpensive and can be replaced, but you boys shouldn't have been throwing pillows in the living room."

"And you shouldn't talk to my boys that way," his gooped-up sister-in-law railed at him, scowling and grabbing hold of Robbie's hand. "It was an accident."

Ted felt his dander rise. "Accident? You call throwing pillows in a living room at midnight an accident? If they wanted to roughhouse, they should have waited till tomorrow and taken it outside. That's what my parents always told me."

Her eyes narrowing, she glared at him. "Maybe that's the reason you and your brother are so messed up. Your parents never let you play like normal children."

"Us messed up? Since my brother has been married to you, he's changed from a happy-go-lucky, carefree guy to an introverted scarecrow of a man who rarely speaks."

"What do you know about marriage? You can't even find a wife!" she flung back.

If Ted hadn't been so upset with the woman, he might

have laughed. Standing in the middle of his living room in his pajamas and her in her tattered robe with that green stuff smeared all over her angry face made him think of a cartoon he'd once seen. He sucked in a breath and faced her again, this time his voice soft and low. "Look, Wilma—I'm sorry for what I said. I know it's hard on all of you with Albert out of a job and having to move in here with me, but it's hard on me, too. Since I've been out on my own, I've never lived with anyone else. Having your family here is an adjustment for me, as well."

Wilma turned in a huff, dragging her sons toward the bedroom they shared. "We'll find another place to live," she called out over her shoulder, her voice continuing to hold its angry edge. "And don't worry about your precious lamp. As soon as Albert gets a job, we'll pay you for it."

"Forget it. It was only a lamp, an object for supplying light. I shouldn't have gotten so upset about it."

As he crouched, grabbed the wastebasket from under his desk, and began to pick up the remains of the lamp, his thoughts went to the lovely, soft-spoken woman with whom he'd spent the day. And he wondered, if he were married to her, or someone like her, would life be wedded bliss? Or, in time, would it, too, lose its luster and turn as sour as his brother's marriage seemed to be?

❧

Since her mother had volunteered to keep the children overnight, Sammy decided to take advantage of the time by playing the CDs a friend from her church had loaned her and doing some much-needed cleaning in the kitchen. But as she listened to a Southern gospel artist sing her favorite songs, visions of the handsome man she'd met on the riverboat filled her thoughts. Why hadn't she asked his last name? Or given him hers? Not that it would make any difference. He probably had no further interest in her anyway, and she'd never go after a man, no matter how nice he seemed, even if he shared her faith. It wasn't her style. She might have done something that gutsy when she was younger, before it became obvious her heart wasn't going to last much longer, but not now. Especially not now.

Now, as far as she was concerned, she was damaged goods, and very few men would want her if they knew. It was a subject she'd rarely discussed with anyone. She'd warned her friends that talking about her heart transplant was forbidden. The last thing she wanted was to be pitied, pampered, and looked at as an invalid who needed special attention. Her deepest desire was to live a healthy life, as normal as possible, for whatever days God allotted her before taking her home to be with Him.

It would be nice to see Ted again, though. We had such a great time together. But I have to face reality. Having a good time with him doesn't give me reason to believe our newfound friendship could develop into something more serious. She pulled a can of cleanser from beneath the sink and began scrubbing at the rust stains around the drain. *But maybe, if I could find him again, the two of us could simply be good friends. Spend time together. A lot of relationships never get past the friendship stage. Isn't that the purpose of dating? To get to know a person before a real relationship develops?*

Her thoughts sounded reasonable and would maybe work with someone else, but she might as well forget about their working for her. The likelihood of the two of them running into each other, even in a city Nashville's size, was pretty slim. *There might be a way, though.* She smiled to herself. *Maybe I could set my apartment on fire, and he'd be one of the firemen to respond.*

"I should be so lucky," she reminded herself aloud with a giggle. "With all the fire stations in town and Ted working only one out of every three days, the odds he'd be one of the responders are definitely not in my favor."

Sammy mentally pictured Ted dressed in his uniform, fire extinguisher in hand, rushing into her apartment to put out the fire and rescue her. "I have to forget about that man. Even if I could find him and he was as interested in spending time with me as I am with him, he'd be repelled by this scar on my chest. Besides, he'd be freaked out to discover the remainder of my life span may be no more than that of a Labrador retriever, not to mention the three children living with me. Hadn't he mentioned his brother's kids drove him crazy and made him decide he didn't want kids?"

As she always did when she felt frustrated and needed to talk to someone about it, Sammy lifted her face heavenward. *Father, it looks as if I already have three strikes against me, and I'm not even up to bat yet! Help!*

Pulling the stopper from the sink, Sammy watched her dreams disappear as they circled down the drain with the bubbles.

three

Sammy's mother arrived at nine the next morning with all three children showered, dressed, and ready for Sunday school. "They were little darlings," she told her. "Even Simon. Your father and I enjoyed having them spend the night. We'll have to do it more often. So how did your day go?"

Before answering, Sammy kissed each child, reminded them she loved them, then sent them off to watch cartoons until time to leave. "It was nice, really nice. Thanks, Mom, for keeping the kids for me."

"You don't have to thank me, sweetie. I just wish we could have them more often. Did you take that ride on the riverboat as you'd planned?"

She smiled. "Yes, it was a wonderful ride. I can't believe I'd never gone on it before. Someday I'll take the children. They'd love it. Maybe, if Dad feels like it, you two can come with us."

"I'm sure we'd enjoy it, but wasn't it kind of lonely? Being by yourself like that? You should have invited one of the women from your Sunday school class to go with you."

Sammy wondered how much she should say. Her mother was such a worrywart, but she had to tell her about Ted. "I—I wasn't exactly alone. I met someone. We had a marvelous day together."

Smiling, her mother grabbed her arm. "Oh, sweetie, I'm so glad. Was she your age? What was she like?"

"She wasn't a she."

"I don't understand. What do you mean?"

"She was a he." Feeling slightly ridiculous at the choice of words she'd used, Sammy muffled a snicker. "I mean, the person I met wasn't a woman. He was a man."

Her mother frowned. "You spent the day with a man? Oh, honey, I've heard of guys who go places like that in search of vulnerable women."

"I'm not as vulnerable as you think, but don't worry. I didn't give him my full name or address." *But I wish I had. I'd like to see him again.* She took hold of her mother's arm and leaned close to her. "He was so nice, Mom. You would have loved him. He's a fireman."

Her mother's eyes widened. "Aren't you the girl who—not to long ago—told me—"

"That no man would ever want me? Yes, and I still feel that way, but I can't tell you how nice it was to be with a man like Ted. He's—"

"Ted? That's his name?"

Sammy felt a flush rise to her cheeks. "Yes, Ted. In some ways he reminds me of Dad. Not that he looks like him, but in other ways. He even called his cheesecake 'tasty.' Dad is the only other man I know who uses that term."

"You don't know many men," her mother reminded her.

"But, Mom, he's kind and gentle, considerate—"

"Maybe he was that way to impress you."

"No, Ted was for real. I could tell," Sammy snapped back, slightly miffed that her mother doubted her words.

"I'd love to see you find a nice man, but you were only on the boat with this stranger for how long? Maybe five or six hours? What makes you think *you* know him that well? He could be an ax murderer for all you know. At least a stalker. I just want you to be careful, that's all."

Rather than argue about it, Sammy lifted her hands in surrender. "You may be right, and I appreciate your concern, but my female intuition tells me otherwise. I wish you could have met him; then you'd understand why I liked him. I think he liked me, too."

"Of course he liked you. You're a lovely person." Her mother's eyes narrowed. "You're sure you didn't give him your phone number or address?"

"Yes, I'm sure. As I said, we didn't even exchange last names."

Mrs. Samuel sighed with relief. "Good, then maybe he won't be able to find you."

"I wish he *could* find me," Sammy whispered so softly her mother couldn't hear. "If only I'd been like Cinderella and left my slipper behind."

❧

"Hey, you. Ted Benay. Get your head out of that newspaper. Lunch is ready."

Ted looked up from the sports section of the Sunday morning paper and smiled at Captain Grey. "Thanks, Cap. Just checking on the Titans. They're having a pretty good season this year."

"About time. With all the muscle power that team has, they should finish in the top three, maybe even higher. Of course, they have to get that quarterback settled down. The guy's too unpredictable. Up one game, down the next. I'd like to see them go all the way to the play-offs, but then I'm biased."

Ted followed his captain down the hall toward the fire station's dining area. "Guess I'm kinda biased, too. I sure wish I could attend all their games."

"Hey, Benay, whatcha think about those Titans?"

Ted smiled at a man already seated at the table then, after nodding at the other guys at the big table, scooted in beside him. "They're doin' real good. You watch that game Monday night?"

"Yeah, that was some game all right. Wasn't that pass McGregor made something? Went right into his receiver's hands slick as a whistle." Reaching across the table, Ted's co-worker grabbed the bowl of mashed potatoes and scooped out a big spoonful, plopping it onto his plate with a snap of his wrist. "Did you see Arkansas play yesterday?"

"Naw, I was, ah, busy."

"Finally got those new hubcaps put on your truck, huh?"

Ted took the bowl from his hands. "Nope, put those on last week. I did something I've wanted to do for a long time— took a ride on the *General Jackson* riverboat."

"Sounds like fun. My wife's been bugging me to take her on that thing." He nudged Ted's arm with his elbow. "You take some purty little gal with you?"

Ted nonchalantly spooned a scoop of potatoes onto his own plate then doused them with a ladle full of thick brown gravy. "Yeah, I guess you could say that."

Jake, one of the guys who loved to needle Ted every chance he had, reared back with a boisterous laugh. "Hey, Benay, you actually had a date? What was the occasion?"

Ted grabbed up a biscuit and pelted the man with it, hitting him on the nose.

Chuckling, the man picked up the pieces and disposed of them in his empty coffee cup. "Good shot!"

Cal, one of Ted's favorite firemen, reached for the platter, took off a luscious-looking piece of fried chicken then passed it on to the next man. "Come on, Ted. 'Fess up. Did you really take some gal on that riverboat? Enquiring minds want to know."

"No, I didn't *take* anyone with me. I went alone when my friend had to cancel on me at the last minute. But I did meet someone, a really nice woman."

"Ted's—got—a—girlfriend," Jake sang in singsong fashion, making up his tune as he went.

"And—it's—about—time," a second man joined in, albeit off-key, as they laughed and jeered at Ted's expense. But he didn't mind. The men he worked with had become like family. He knew they meant well.

Jake speared a piece of chicken then handed Ted the platter. "So you picked up some little gal on the boat?"

Ted wished he'd kept his mouth shut and let them think he'd gone alone and stayed that way. They constantly teased him about being the most eligible bachelor on his shift and challenged him to go out and find himself a woman. Though he didn't mind the teasing, he hated having to explain himself.

"I didn't pick her up, as you so crudely put it, Jake. We just sort of ended up sitting next to each other. That's all. I don't even know her last name." *But I wish I did!*

"But you got her phone number, right?"

Ted turned toward Cal who was shoveling food into his mouth as if it were his last meal. "No, I didn't."

Jake snorted. "Either you were a fool, or she was a real dog. Which was it?"

"Fool, I guess. She was one of the nicest, prettiest women I've ever met, and I let her get away. I have no idea how to find her."

The laughter ceased as every man eyed Ted.

"You're serious?"

Ted nodded. "Yeah, Cal, I'm dead serious. As we were getting off the boat, I ran into one of my friends, and he wanted to introduce me to his family. In the confusion of everyone heading for the gangway, I lost Sammy in the crowd. By the time I got to the exit gate, she was already gone."

Jake wiped his chin with his napkin. "Bummer. Too bad, guy. Next time make it a priority to at least get the gal's phone number."

"I'd hoped to hear from her, but so far she hasn't called me."

"You gave her *your* number? That was pretty smart. Maybe you're not as dumb as we thought you were."

Ted sent Cal a feeble smile. "You give me too much credit. I didn't give her my number, at least not directly." He explained about the jacket and leaving his number with the lady at the ticket office. "I'm hoping she'll call."

"There're plenty of fish in the sea, Ted," Captain Grey said sympathetically. "If one gets away, there's always another."

Again Jake snorted. "Yeah, but some of those fish are scrawny little unattractive minnows who aren't the kind you want to keep; some are pretty trout and the best fish a man could catch"—he paused for effect—"and some are dangerous piranhas, the kind you should stay away from, unless you're lookin' for big trouble. From my experience, that sea of women has far more piranhas in it than trout. You might want to throw the minnows back. The piranhas may be pretty, but don't forget they're deadly. The trout? When you find one of those babies you know you've hit pay dirt. From the stars in old Teddy-boy's eyes, I'd say the one he let get away was a trout. If it was me, I'd keep right on fishing in that same sea until I found her again."

Ted pondered his words. No doubt about it, the fish he'd hoped would end up in his net had, through his own carelessness, gotten away. That jacket was the only bait he had to find her. But the sad thing was, unless the ticket office lady gave Sammy his number and she called him, he had no idea where to fish.

"Hey, Cal, you gonna eat those mashed potatoes all by yourself, or are you gonna share that bowl with the rest of us?" Before Cal could respond with a snappy retort or shove the potatoes in Jake's direction, the alarm sounded, and the dispatcher's voice boomed vital information throughout the station. Every man headed toward the fire trucks and their waiting gear, leaving their half-eaten lunch on the table.

ða

Sammy stuck her arm out of the covers long enough to hit the snooze button when the alarm went off at its usual time on Monday morning. "Just five more minutes, please," she groaned, turning over on her side. "I'm not ready to get up yet."

When the shrill sound ripped through her bedroom a second time, she begrudgingly flipped off the covers, stood, and went through her usual waking-up routine, stretching first one arm then the other, then bending and touching her toes. Like it or not, it was time to face the day. She decided she had time to add a load of dirty weekend laundry to the washing machine before putting breakfast together. She quickly emptied both hers and the children's hampers and began sorting things into piles by color when it occurred to her that her jacket was missing. She'd purposely taken it with her on the riverboat, but where was it now? Had she left it in the car? No, she would have seen it when she'd gone to church.

Disgusted with herself, she shook her head. *I left it on the riverboat. I hope someone turned it in, or they found it when they cleaned the upper deck.* She glanced at her watch. *Too early to call now. I'll call them later.*

"Up, up, up!" She clapped her hands then gently tugged off the quilts that covered the three little munchkins with whom she shared her apartment. Getting two children off to school, little Harley to the babysitter, and herself ready for work each morning was no easy task. "Rise and shine, kidlings. Open those little eyes."

By ten o'clock, with everyone safely deposited in their proper places, Sammy picked up the phone on her office desk and called the riverboat ticket office.

"Yes, someone did bring in a jacket that had been left on the upper deck last Saturday. He left his name and number on a piece of paper, said for you to call and he'd bring the jacket by your apartment," the woman explained.

Sammy's heart soared. Ted had left his number?

"I taped it up here on the wall by the phone"—the woman paused—"but it's gone now. Don't know what happened to it, but since he was a friend of yours, I guess you know the number."

Her heart plummeted as quickly as it had risen. "No, I don't know it. If he calls again, would you have him call me? I'd like to get my jacket back." *And I want to see him again.*

"Sure—give me your number. This time I'll write it on the inside cover of our phone book so it won't get lost."

Though Sammy gave the woman both her home and work numbers, she doubted Ted would call the riverboat again. When she didn't call him, he'd probably think either the jacket wasn't of value to her or she didn't want to see him again, or both. She thanked the woman then hung up. It seemed her life was one long series of ups and downs.

Mostly downs.

Her thoughts still filled with visions of the handsome fireman, she tried to imagine what it would be like to date Ted. Maybe even marry him. She'd be Mrs. Ted—ah—what? She didn't even know his full name. And though he had a great personality, was well mannered, and seemed like an all-around nice guy, was he a Christian? Did he share her faith? To her, that would be the most important part of any relationship.

❧

Two weeks passed, and the phone call from Sammy didn't come. Though Ted had nearly given up on hearing from her, each time he passed his closet he couldn't resist opening the door and glancing at her jacket.

Another week went by. Still no call.

"Hey, Benay, what happened to that girl you met on the riverboat?" Without even turning, Ted knew it was Jake. "She give you the boot? Find herself another boyfriend?"

Ted shrugged. "We kinda lost track of each other."

"I got the impression you really liked that girl," his captain chimed in.

"I did."

"And you're going to give up on her, just like that?"

"I didn't exactly give up on her."

"She dumped you, right?"

Ted swung around toward Cal. "No, she didn't dump me. I think she actually liked me."

Jake waved the popcorn bowl in Ted's face. "If she liked you and you say you haven't given up on her, what's your problem?"

"I hoped she'd call, but—"

The alarm went off for the third time in less than two hours, ending their conversation and sending the men scurrying toward the truck.

"I'm thankful it isn't that nursing home again," Cal yelled out over the sound of the motor as Jake revved up the truck's big engine. "I love those old people, but I sure hate it when we can't help them or we're too late."

Like two others they'd had in the past two hours, the call was a near false alarm. The fire was out by the time they got there. All it had taken was a neighbor's borrowed fire extinguisher to put out the small fire that had started in a garage.

"You'd think people would invest a few bucks in a home fire extinguisher," Cal quipped with disgust, sliding out of his boots and outer pants and then placing them next to the fire truck. "They invest most of their income in their home and its contents but won't buy an extinguisher."

Jake gave his arm a playful nudge. "Why should they when they have us? Most folks think all we do is watch TV and play dominoes. Face it, man. We've got the kind of job most men only dream about."

Cal rose quickly as the shrill alarm sounded again, echoing throughout the station. "There she goes! We've got another one. Surely it's not another false alarm."

Ted felt a rush of adrenaline as he pulled on his pants, boots, and jacket and swung himself up into his seat. Maybe it was the fear of the unknown, the anticipation of putting out the fire and keeping everyone safe. Whatever it was, the thrill of being a firefighter was always there, surging through his blood, and he loved every minute of it. It was as if his calling in life had been to be a fireman.

Within three minutes, they pulled up in front of one of the larger office buildings in their district and began their standard procedures. The police arrived on the scene at nearly the same time and took charge of the scores of employees who were rushing out of the building in a panic.

"It's in the furnace room!" shouted a man who looked to be one of the building's maintenance crew, pointing to the back of the large building. "Not sure what caused it, but it's really burning in there!"

The engine from another fire company pulled up, followed by a third engine. Knowing exactly what to do and how to do it, the firemen from the three companies worked together until the fire was out. It wasn't as serious as they'd first thought, but if they hadn't arrived when they did, with that many people working in the building, it could have been a lot more serious.

⁂

Sammy stood on the sidewalk, her heart pounding in her ears, her hands trembling. She'd never been in a building when it caught on fire. Just the sound of the fire alarm going off had terrified her. Along with the other people who worked there, she'd made her way down the stairwell and out onto the street, watching in amazement as the firemen methodically went about their business.

Tiffany, her company's receptionist, poked her in the arm as they stood a half hour later watching the activity playing out before them. "Aren't they cute in their uniforms?"

Sammy blinked hard. "The firemen?"

Tiffany nodded then popped her gum. "Yeah, the firemen. Who'd you think I meant? Wonder if they'd let me take one of those guys home with me? Maybe that one over there. The tall one. He'd look real fine in my apartment."

Sammy turned to see which man Tiffany was talking about. "I don't know how you could tell. In those uniforms, they all look alike."

Tiffany let out a chuckle. "No problem. I'd take any one of them, sight unseen."

I'd take one of them, too, if his name were Ted.

The young woman ran her fingers through her bleached, spiked hair then tugged at her short skirt. "Come on, Sammy. Don't tell me you wouldn't like to have one of those hunky guys living in *your* apartment. Surely you have blood flowing through those veins of yours."

Sammy hoped her thoughts about Ted hadn't made her blush but then realized the fast trip down the stairs had already done that job. "If he was the right guy I would, but only if we were married."

Tiffany wrinkled up her face then popped her gum again. "Right guy? Surely you don't believe in that one-special-man-created-just-for-you stuff."

Sammy hadn't expected to get into this type of conversation while standing in the parking lot surrounded by fire trucks and police cars, but she had to let this young woman know where she stood. "Yes, Tiffany, I do believe that. I don't know if God intended for me to marry or not, but if He did I'm sure He has the right man out there—somewhere."

Tiffany sighed, her long chandelier earrings swaying from side to side like the pendulum on a clock. "How're you going to find him? The world is full of men."

"I don't know how, but God can bring us together. I'm sure of it."

"Meantime you're gonna save yourself for him? That special man you're expecting God to send you with a sign on his back saying he's yours?"

Sammy didn't like the ridiculing tone of Tiffany's voice or the way she was making fun of something of vital importance to her. But the girl was young and more interested in men than she was in God's will for her life, so Sammy answered as kindly as she could. "That's exactly what I'm going to do, and I hope he's saving himself for me."

Tiffany's eyes widened. "That's about the most absurd statement I've ever heard. You really think some guy is saving himself for you? Maybe they did stuff like that in the Dark Ages but not in today's world. If you want a man, you've got to do like the rest of us. Go out there and find him. Go where men congregate. Pick out one you like. Flirt, throw yourself at him—do whatever it takes to get his attention."

Sammy crossed her arms over her chest and scrunched up her face. "No, thanks. I'd never be that desperate."

"Are you insinuating I'm desperate?"

"I'm not insinuating anything, Tiffany. I'm simply telling you how I feel."

An officer moved up between them and motioned toward the double doors. "You ladies can go back into the building now. Everything is under control."

Relieved at having a reason to bring their awkward conversation to an end, Sammy turned in the man's direction. But it wasn't his face that caught her attention; it was the familiar face of a fireman standing alongside one of the big red vehicles.

"Ted?"

four

Cal jabbed Ted in the shoulder as the two stood by the fire truck waiting for their captain to come back from his final walk-through. "Hey, old buddy, you get a load of all those good-lookin' women standing over there by those double doors?"

Ted sent him an amused grin. "Nope. Never noticed."

"Man, you'd better get yourself to the doc for a checkup as soon as possible. Somethin's wrong with you. You're not still pining over that little gal you met on the riverboat, are you?"

Ted snorted, not about to tell Cal that Sammy was the subject of nearly all of his waking thoughts and sometimes his dreams. "Only thing wrong with me is I'm too picky. I don't want just any woman; I want the right woman."

"You ain't gonna find her sittin' on your duff. You gotta get out there and circulate." Cal latched onto Ted's arm. "Why don't I take you over there and introduce you to one of those pretty gals?"

Ted let out a chuckle. "You don't know any of those women."

"Hey, don't need to know them. Women are always impressed with a man in uniform. I guarantee you—if the two of us walked over there and said hello, we'd have those women falling all over us. I'd even give you first choice."

Ted frowned. "And then you'd pick one? I don't think that

sweet little wife of yours would approve."

Cal wiggled his eyebrows. "I won't tell if you don't."

With a roll of his eyes, Ted tugged his arm away. He hated it when the married guys at his station talked that way, even if they didn't mean it. "You go wow them if you want. I'll stay and finish up here."

Cal shrugged. "Don't say I didn't offer. Man, if I was your age and as good-lookin' as you, I'd—"

"Ted?"

Ted glanced up at the sound of his name.

It was Sammy!

It was actually Sammy!

Without a word of explanation to Cal, Ted hurried over to her. But when they met halfway, he stopped. He wanted to take her in his arms and hang on tight; he wasn't about to lose her a second time. But, being a gentleman and not wanting to come on too strong and frighten the poor girl, he simply gazed down at her awkwardly, his arms dangling at his sides. "Hi," he finally managed to say. "I've been thinking about you." She was every bit as attractive as the first time he'd met her.

Sammy gazed up at him. "I've been thinking about you, too."

"I tried to catch you that day, but by the time my friends and I left the boat, you were already gone. I'd hoped you'd wait for me."

"I—I didn't want to intrude. And, after all, our ride was over. One of the crew members opened the gate and motioned for all of us to exit, so I just moved along with the crowd."

Though he didn't want to stare, he couldn't help himself. Her shoulder-length brown hair glistened in the sun, and her eyes, as blue as he'd remembered them, held him captive. "I found your jacket."

"I know. I called the ticket office. They told me you'd taken it with you, but somehow the note with your phone number on it disappeared from the wall where the lady had taped it. I didn't know how to reach you."

"I didn't know how to reach you either. I—I still have your jacket. It's hanging in my hall closet. I could bring it to you." *Get her phone number and address and her last name!*

"That's asking too much of you. Why don't I come by the fire station and pick it up?"

He was tempted to say yes so his firefighting buddies would know he truly had met a real live girl on that riverboat. But he wasn't taking any chances. He wanted to make sure he could find her again. "No, give me your address. It'd be a lot simpler if I brought it to you."

Though her smile lingered, Ted noticed that she pulled back slightly at his suggestion. "Or maybe we could have lunch tomorrow, and I could bring it to you there," he added quickly. "You name the place."

⁂

Sammy's heart raced. Wonder of wonders! The fantastic man she'd met on the riverboat was standing in front of her, and he was asking her to meet him for lunch. She was glad he'd suggested lunch. She didn't know him well enough to invite him up to her apartment or go to his. "That's a great idea, Ted. I do need to get my jacket back. There's a terrific soup and sandwich shop about a block down from here. Maybe we could meet there. About noon?" His smile made her heart flutter.

"I know the place. Noon would be great."

"But it has to be my treat. After all, you are returning my jacket."

His smile broadened. "I'll arm wrestle you for the check. But I warn you, firemen are good arm wrestlers. It's an Olympic sport at the station."

She loved his warm smile, his boyish ways, and his sense of humor. They were what had attracted her to him in the first place. "No way! I appreciate your taking care of my jacket. It's one of my favorites. The least I can do is buy you lunch." Sammy hoped she wasn't grinning like some starstruck teenager, but she was so glad she'd found him, and not just because she wanted her jacket back.

"Hey, Ted. We're ready to roll."

"Sorry. Got to rush off. The captain is ready. See you tomorrow?" Sending her another grin, he backed away.

"Yeah, tomorrow. 'Bye."

" 'Bye."

Sammy watched until he'd climbed into the cab and the big truck disappeared around the corner before heading back into the building, her heart doing cartwheels. Ted was back in her life, even if only for one more day, and she still didn't know his last name.

She took care of a number of customer service calls the next morning, but time seemed to stand still. Sammy found herself checking the clock every five minutes. At eleven thirty, purse in hand, she headed for the ladies' room to comb her hair and freshen up her lipstick.

As she passed the reception desk in her company's foyer, Tiffany popped her chewing gum, then cocked her head to one side and gave her a once-over. "You're lookin' good today, girl. Where you going? The man upstairs call you from heaven and tell you that special man He created for you was waiting here in the lobby to take you to lunch?"

Unable to resist, Sammy donned a big smile. "You should know. Wouldn't God have had to go through your switchboard to reach me? What's the matter? Didn't you recognize His voice?"

Apparently unfazed by her question, Tiffany smiled at her. "Next time you talk to that God of yours, ask Him to send me a man about six foot tall, black hair, blue eyes, with a great personality and lots of money. Tell Him if He does, I'll go to church on Sunday."

Sammy gave her a wink then hurried toward the double doors, calling back over her shoulder, "Too bad you didn't recognize His voice. You could have asked Him yourself."

Despite the time it took for her little repartee with Tiffany, Sammy was still five minutes early when she strolled into the soup and sandwich shop. Ted was already there and seated at a booth near the wall.

"Over here!" Rising, a grin broke out across his face. "I got here early."

She smiled a hello then noticed her jacket neatly folded on the opposite side of the booth and seated herself next to it. "I'm early, too."

He picked up a menu and handed it to her. "I know you like iced tea. I've already ordered it for you. I hope that's okay."

"Iced tea is fine." She gestured toward her jacket. "Thanks for bringing it, Ted. I was afraid it was lost forever when they couldn't find the phone number you'd left."

"I thought I'd lost you—" He lowered his gaze and almost

seemed nervous. "I mean, without your phone number or last name, I had no idea how to reach you—to give you back your jacket."

The waitress arrived with two tall glasses of iced tea. "What'll you have, folks?"

Sammy closed the menu and handed it to her. "I'll have the Minnie Pearl, please."

Ted looked up from his menu. "The Minnie Pearl? What's that?"

She reached across the table and pointed to a spot at the far right side of his menu. "I guess you haven't had a chance to look at it yet. Every item on the menu is named for a country music star. The Minnie Pearl is actually broccoli cheese soup and a small shaved ham sandwich. I order it nearly every time I come here."

Ted scrunched up his face and stared at the vast array of selections. "Um, let me see. I guess—I'll have—the Garth Brooks."

Sammy had to laugh. "Oh, you like Reuben sandwiches, too? The Garth Brooks is my second favorite."

"Great minds think alike!"

"Mind if I pray?" she asked when their lunch arrived.

"I'd be disappointed if you didn't."

What did that mean? Slightly confused by his answer, she bowed her head and uttered a quick thank-You-for-our-food prayer before picking up her spoon and plunging it into her soup.

They laughed their way through lunch, talking about the way they'd met, the fun they'd had on the riverboat, her jacket, and the uncanny way they'd met again at the fire.

"I can't let you pay for my lunch," Sammy told him, reaching for her purse when the waitress brought the check.

"Oh, so you do want to arm wrestle me for it. I'm only kidding. Put your money away. No woman I take to lunch is going to pick up her tab. My daddy raised me right."

Though she felt awkward letting him pay for her lunch, she was impressed by his determination to do what he considered the gallant thing. Actually she considered it gallant, too.

"Looks like we were destined to meet," Ted told her as he walked her back to her building. "Don't you think it's about time we officially introduced ourselves?" He reached out his hand. "I'm Ted Benay. Nashville firefighter extraordinaire."

Sammy smiled up at him. "Hi, Ted Benay. I'm Sammy Samuel. Waggoner Enterprise's super-experienced customer service director."

He raised his brow. "How about giving me your phone number? I'd like to give you a call sometime. Like maybe tomorrow when I'm at the station."

Why not? What harm could it do? She gave him a bashful grin. How long had it been since a man had asked for her phone number? "It's 555-2172."

Ted patted his shirt pocket. "I don't have a pen."

"I have one." Sammy unzipped the clutch bag she carried to work each day and fished around inside, pulling out a small spiral pad. "Um, a pad, but no pen. I must have left it on my desk."

"That's okay. I have a good memory. You did say five-five-five—twenty-one-seventy-two, right?"

"You do have a good memory. That's exactly right." After sliding the pad back inside, she zipped the bag shut.

He opened one of the double doors to her building then tipped his imaginary hat. "Thank you for the pleasure of your company, Sammy Samuel. I'll call you tomorrow."

"And thank you for a pleasant lunch, Ted Benay. I'll look forward to your call."

"Any special time be best?"

Remembering how noisy it was in her apartment before the children went to bed, she considered his question carefully. "Best after nine in the evening. I'm—busy—before then."

He tipped his imaginary hat again. "Nine it is."

She felt his eyes pinned on her as she moved through the open door and toward the elevator. Could this really be happening? Could this handsome man be interested in her enough to call her? *Calm down, girl. He was only talking about a single phone call, not a long-term commitment. Don't get your hopes up. You may never hear from him again. And at this point you're not even sure he's a Christian.*

"Well, you're looking rosy." Tiffany's voice carried its usual mocking tone as Sammy passed the reception desk. "That must have been some lunch, or did you drink too much wine?"

Sammy hated to dignify Tiffany's comment with an answer, but she felt she needed to respond. "The lunch was terrific. No wine needed. And, yes, God sent that special man to take me to lunch." *I hope it was God who sent him.* "He's a fantastic guy. Maybe someday I'll bring him to the office so you can meet him, but you have to promise—hands off! He's mine." *I can't believe I actually said that! Now she'll be expecting me to bring Ted here.*

Tiffany's face sobered. "You're serious? A man really did take you to lunch?"

"Of course a man did. A real hunk of a guy." Sammy lifted her chin and put on a mischievous smile then headed for her office, leaving Tiffany with her mouth hanging open.

⁂

The next evening nine o'clock came, then nine thirty, then ten, and still no call from Ted. He'd seemed so sincere when he'd promised to call. Sammy fingered the tip of her scar. Surely he hadn't noticed it. As was her custom, she'd worn a high-necked blouse. *Maybe he's too busy to call.* She shook her head to clear her thoughts. Why was she making excuses for him? He hadn't called as he'd said he would, plain and simple. She'd been a fool to believe she'd ever hear from him again.

⁂

Ted stared at the phone. How could he have forgotten Sammy's number? He'd been so sure he'd remembered it correctly; yet each of the three times he'd dialed it, the same man had answered the phone, obviously irritated. Great! Sammy was expecting his call, and he had no way to reach her. He tried checking the phone book, but either her number was unlisted or listed under another name. If he had her address, he would go right over there and tell her his addled brain had somehow transposed her number. But, since he didn't know it, he could only wait until morning and try to catch her at her office.

He arrived shortly after nine at the reception desk. "I'd like to see Sammy Samuel, please."

Popping her gum, the receptionist gave him a sideways tilt of her head and blinked her long lashes seductively. "You the guy who took her to lunch the other day?"

Startled by her question and wondering how she knew, Ted

frowned. "Yeah, I am. Would you please call her and tell her I'm here?"

"Be happy to." The flirtatious smile she gave him as she picked up the phone made him uncomfortable. "Wait here."

Within seconds of her call, Sammy appeared, looking businesslike in pretty dark blue pants and a white shirt. Ted felt as tongue-tied as a schoolboy as he gazed at her. Something about her was different. Her hair, maybe? Whatever it was, she looked good.

"Well, hello. I didn't expect to see you here this morning." She eyed him a bit coolly and then, after a glance in the receptionist's direction, motioned toward two chairs along the wall. "We can talk over there."

Once they were seated, Ted smiled, hoping she wasn't upset that he hadn't called as he'd said he would. "You must think I'm a real dodo. I thought sure I'd remember your phone number, but somehow I got it messed up. Some man kept answering, and he was none too happy." He grinned. "I really wanted to talk to you last night. All I can say is I'm sorry."

Her face softened into a demure smile. "I thought maybe you didn't mean it when you said you'd call."

"Oh, I intended to call you all right. I just didn't know how." Ted couldn't keep his eyes off her. It seemed each time he saw her, she was more beautiful than the last. "I have to know something, Sammy. Do you have a steady boyfriend? Are you engaged? Married?" What a dumb thing to come right out and ask, but he had to know. He was attracted to this woman, but he sure didn't want to tread on some decent man's toes.

She burst out laughing at his impromptu question. "No, none of the above. Are you?"

"Am I what?"

"Married or engaged or have a steady girlfriend?"

"Oh, I get it. Turnabout is fair play, true? I guess you have as much right to know the answer to those questions as I do. Like you, none of the above!" He never blushed, so why did his cheeks feel hot?

❦

Sammy froze as Ted reached his hand across and cupped hers.

"I enjoyed our time together on the *General Jackson*. If I'd had my wits about me and gotten your address, I would have sent you flowers to show my appreciation for allowing me to share your day with you."

Be still, my heart. "I had a great time, too, but as much as I love flowers, you needn't have sent them. You barely know me."

He gave her hand a gentle squeeze. "Not by choice. I'd planned on inviting you out to dinner so I *could* get to know you. But, dumb me, I left you standing on the deck when I ran into my friend and his family and let you get away. Do you think you could ever forgive me?" A grin tilting at his lips, he let go of her hand and shifted his body toward the edge of his seat. "I'll even get down on my knees and beg your forgiveness if it'll help."

"No, don't! I mean, there's nothing to forgive. We'd just met. You owed me nothing. I'm the one with the debt. I owe you for taking care of my jacket."

His face brightened. "Does that mean if I asked you out on a real date, you'd accept?"

She nibbled at her lip, fighting the gigantic smile that begged to erupt. He was asking her for a date! "What kind of date?"

"Dinner at a nice place, then a movie. A chick flick, if that's the kind you like. Hot fudge sundae at the ice cream parlor afterward. Whatever you want to do. Wherever you want to go. Your choice."

His hand cupped hers again. It felt warm. Safe. Strong. "I do like you, Ted," she began, wondering if she should blurt out the reasons that would send him running the other way if he knew her background and what her life was like or if she should drag it out slowly. "And I'd love to accept your invitation, but—"

"But what? I promise I'm trustworthy. We can even take someone with us if you're concerned about going out alone with me when you don't know me any better than you do."

She swallowed hard. "It isn't that I don't know you. It's that *you* don't know me."

His grip tightened on her hand. "That's the whole point of it, Sammy. That's why you should go to dinner with me. I want to get to know you. I'm sure there's nothing you could tell me that would make me *not* want to know you better. I have a feeling you and I think alike."

"I'd like to go—really I would—but there's—"

With a teasing smile, , he put his finger on her lips. "Shh, not another word. If either of us has any skeletons in our closets, we'll deal with them later. But at this moment, let's concentrate on the here and now." He laughed. "Who knows? Maybe once we get to know each other, we won't like one another and won't even have to deal with those skeletons."

Sammy evaluated his words carefully. Though he was saying it in jest, what he was saying was true. Maybe they wouldn't like each other, but it would be fun dating him to find out.

And he was a great guy. What harm could it do? She didn't have to tell him about the children now and certainly not that she had a transplanted heart. And she was sure her next-door neighbor would stay with the children if she asked her. "Okay, if your invitation still stands, I'd love to have dinner with you." From the look on his face, it seemed he was as pleased with her answer as she was.

"Thursday night work for you? Unless you'd rather go someplace else, how about having dinner at the Opryland Hotel?"

Her heart raced with excitement. "Isn't it a bit pricey?"

"Have you ever eaten there?"

"No, believe it or not, I've never even been in the hotel, but I've heard it's nice."

"You've never been to the Opryland Hotel? Then I have to take you there. That's where I took my mom for Mother's Day, and she loved it. What time shall I pick you up?"

Pick me up? "Maybe I could just meet you somewhere."

"Hey, this is an official date, remember?"

"Yes, I remember. Would seven be okay? That'll give me time to get home from work and change into something more suitable." Her heart pounded against her chest. Perhaps she could have her neighbor keep the kids over in her apartment for the evening so he wouldn't be flabbergasted by their presence when she opened the door. Yes, that would work. She'd just have to make sure their toys and belongings weren't left scattered around.

"Seven it is, but you'd better write your address down on a piece of paper along with your phone number. I've already proven how bad my memory is."

After asking Tiffany for a pen and paper, Sammy wrote down the information and handed it to him, watching as he folded it and stuck it in his shirt pocket.

"See you Thursday night at seven." He gave her a slight wave then hurried to catch the elevator before the doors closed.

"Hey, if you don't want that guy, I'll take him. He's cute!"

Sammy tried to appear casual as she made her way past Tiffany's desk, although inside she was a bundle of nerves. "Thanks for the offer, but I think I'll keep him."

"Where'd you meet him? I've never seen him around here before."

Sammy smiled. "Would you believe me if I said God sent him?"

Tiffany's eyes rounded. "You really think He did?"

The smile still etched on her face, Sammy shrugged. "Only God knows the answer to that question."

ঌ

"Thanks, Edna, I owe you one." Sammy closed the door of her neighbor's apartment Thursday evening and then hurried back across the hall to her own apartment.

Her place looked strangely unfamiliar without the toys, books, crayons, and videos that normally adorned her living room. She scanned her surroundings one more time, making sure all the evidence of living with three children had been removed. After one final glance in the hall mirror, she sat down to wait for Ted's arrival. *I actually have a date, a real date, and with a very nice man! I hope I don't spill food or knock my glass over and embarrass myself. Or Ted!*

He arrived on the stroke of seven, a small bouquet of flowers in his hand and the dazzling smile on his face that always made her heart beat faster. "Hi, these are for you."

Sammy clasped her fist against her pounding chest. "Oh, Ted, how thoughtful. I love flowers, but you—"

"Shouldn't have? Ah, but I should. I wanted to. By the way, you sure look nice. I like that scarf thing you have around your neck. Nice colors."

"Thank you. It was a gift from my mom." She fingered the scarf to make sure it was covering what she'd intended. "I'd better put these roses in water so they won't wilt."

When she realized he was following her into the kitchen, she panicked. Had she made sure all traces of kid stuff had been removed from the kitchen? She couldn't remember, but, much to her relief, the kitchen was in perfect order, without a crayon, lunch box, or child-sized garment in sight.

He summed up the area. "Nice place you have here."

"Thanks. It's a little crowded with"—she paused, quickly rethinking her choice of words—"with everything. I can't seem to throw anything away."

His brows rose. "You, too, huh? That's the way I am. Always sure I'll need it again someday."

The traffic was unusually heavy for a Thursday evening as they made their way up Gallatin and turned onto Briley Parkway toward the Music Valley section. "You lived in Nashville long?"

Sammy smiled up at him. "I lived here growing up, left to get an education, took a job in Denver, and moved back here about three years ago, so I guess you could say this is home. How about you?"

"My family moved here before I went into the service, so when I was discharged I decided to come back here. I like

Nashville. It has a lot to offer."

"I think you said you like working as a fireman, right?"

Without taking his eyes off the road, he nodded. "Yeah, I do. Good pay, good benefits, and I like the idea of having one day on and two days off. Good retirement program, too. You said you like being a customer service director, too, didn't you?"

Sammy gazed out the window, taking in the scenery. She rarely got to this part of town. "Yes, I really do. I like working with people and their problems. It's such a great feeling when you're able to solve them and they walk away happy."

"Sounds like a tall order to me. People can be so cantankerous sometimes. I had a woman so mad her face turned red when I had to use the fire extinguisher to put out a fire in her kitchen because of the gray residue it left, and she's the one who called 911 asking for help. Guess some folks you can never please."

"I have one of those occasionally, but most of the people I deal with only want satisfaction. If I'm nice to them, let them know I sincerely care about their problem and can work things out to where they're happy with the solution, they'll stay a customer. That's my goal. I try to tell everyone in my department it's much easier to keep an old customer than it is to find a new one."

"Sounds smart to me." He gestured toward the Opryland Hotel as he turned into the parking lot. "Hope you're hungry."

She allowed a grin to tilt her lips. "Starved."

Since Ted had called in their reservation to the restaurant located in the hotel's atrium, they were taken in right away and seated at a table for two near the railing, overlooking the spectacular cascades and courtyard.

"Wow!" Sammy gazed at each of the two glassed-in walls surrounding them.

"Nice, isn't it? I thought you'd like it."

"Those waterfalls are incredible, and the gardens! I've never seen such lush growth."

"The entire hotel is like this. We'll take a walk around it when we're finished. This area is only a small part of it."

Her gaze wandered upward to the high domed glass ceiling that towered over them and gave light to the thousands of plants. "This is amazing!"

"That it is. I know I was impressed the first time I came here." He handed her a menu then scanned his own. "How about Australian lobster tail for dinner?"

"I've never had lobster tail."

"Then it's settled. You must have it tonight."

They commented on the many iron balconies that clung to the walls around the atrium and discussed the various types of plants in the gardens and a myriad of other things as they munched on their salads and waited for their entrées. Finally their dinners arrived.

Sammy's eyes widened. The lobster smelled delicious and looked phenomenal, but she had no idea how to eat it.

"Madam? May I?"

She looked up into the smiling face of the waiter then nodded as he, tools in hand, poised himself over her dish. She was relieved for him to do what was needed to get to the meat in the lobster tail. Just watching him and his routine was a treat.

But Ted declined when the man offered to assist him.

"Thanks, but I like to do it myself so I can get every tiny morsel. I love this stuff."

"It does look good." As was her habit, Sammy wanted to pray before her meal, but she wasn't sure how he would feel, especially in such a nice restaurant. She sat patiently waiting until their server left. She couldn't help but smile. When she was a child, her grandmother always told her she would get indigestion if she didn't thank the Lord for her food.

"Guess it's my turn to pray. You prayed last time." The words rolled off his tongue as easily as if he'd asked her if she wanted a glass of water. Without waiting, he bowed his head and prayed in a way that let her know he had a personal relationship with God. Ted was a Christian!

After he said amen, Ted waved his fork and gestured toward her plate. "Go ahead. Try it. Take a small piece and dip it in that little container of drawn butter."

Still touched by the way he'd prayed, she did as he'd instructed, being careful not to dribble the warm butter on her chin. "Mmm, it *is* good and so mild. I thought it would taste strong or fishy, but it's not like that at all."

He grinned. "See, I told you you'd like it. Now try the vegetables. They really know how to fix zucchini. I guess it's roasted or something."

"It's delicious," she told him after taking a mouthful. "I've never had it seasoned this way. I like it."

They giggled their way through the rest of the meal, teasing and visiting like old friends.

"How about caramel cheesecake for dessert?"

Her hand on her tummy, Sammy stared at him wide-eyed. "Surely you're kidding. After that meal? No way!"

He lowered his lip and frowned. "Guess that means I can't have any. Next time we come here, we'll have to save room for dessert."

Next time? Did that mean he liked her? That he was truly enjoying her company? She was certainly enjoying his.

They lingered over coffee, and then Ted paid the check. "How about a boat ride?"

She gave him a blank stare. "Now?"

"Yeah, right here in the hotel, complete with a guide. It's not exactly the *General Jackson*, but they have five nice twenty-five-passenger Delta River flatboats. I think you'll like it."

His enthusiasm was contagious.

"A boat ride sounds wonderful."

After strolling through several lighted lush green walkways and over a bridge, they eventually came to the landing where the boats loaded. "They call it an indoor river," Ted explained, taking her hand and helping her into one of the seats. "It winds through the hotel's four-and-a-half-acre indoor garden."

Sammy had never been in such a romantic setting. It was like a movie, and she was the star. Chills ran down her spine when she felt Ted's arm slide around her shoulders and draw her close. She didn't know if she should scoot closer or pull away.

He leaned toward her, his forehead nearly touching hers, and whispered, "You're a great date. I'm sure glad you said yes."

"I'm glad, too. This beautiful hotel, the lobster, now this boat ride." She shivered as she felt his warm breath on her cheek. "This—this has been a magical evening."

"It's been magical for me, too. Good thing you left your jacket on the riverboat. Otherwise I may never have found you."

"I'm glad I left it, too."

"Maybe the man upstairs wanted us to find each other."

Sammy sucked in a deep breath. *The man upstairs? He calls God the man upstairs? I thought he shared my faith!*

"Well, I guess I shouldn't have said 'the man upstairs,'" he went on, apparently oblivious to her repulsion at that name. "I know a lot of folks call God that, but it's disrespectful. I guess I'm around the guys at the fire station so much I automatically pick up their lingo and use it without even thinking sometimes. God is much too important to be called by such a frivolous name."

Though slightly relieved by his explanation, Sammy was reminded of Tiffany's comment. "I know what you mean. I hear that kind of talk every day. God is the most important part of my life. Like you, I hate to hear Him called by that name. It's so disrespectful."

"I won't say it again. To be honest, the Lord is the most important part of my life, too, but right now I'm having trouble understanding His will. He allowed something to happen that changed my life forever, and I'm still struggling to understand why."

"His plan and will for our—"

Frowning, he pulled away a bit. "My mom has given me all those arguments and quoted dozens of scripture verses to me, but I can't see what good could come out of what He allowed to happen." His frown eased, and he smiled as he leaned toward the side of the boat. "If you keep an eye on the water, you might get a glimpse of Danny."

"Danny? Who is Danny?"

Ted laughed. "The hotel's eighty-pound catfish. I'm sure

the guide will be telling us about him soon."

Though Sammy wished their conversation could have continued, she couldn't help but laugh, too. "An eighty-pound catfish? Wow! Now that's a fish." She kept smiling, but inside she was aching for Ted. Something had hurt him—enough to cause him to doubt God's will. What was it?

At that exact moment, the guide began to tell them the story of Danny. "But, folks, I haven't seen Danny all evening. He must be taking a nap."

"Too bad," Ted told her, his gaze scanning the river. "I hoped you'd get to see him." He smiled and pointed. "Around that curve up ahead is Delta Island's eighty-five-foot waterfall. Can you imagine building a place like this?"

"No, I can't. I never dreamed this hotel was so large and so beautiful. I'd like to see it at Christmastime. It must be spectacular."

Ted moved a little closer and gave her a nudge. "We can always come back again. I'm sure the restaurant has other items on its menu we can try."

Sammy gave him a bashful grin. "Come here again? You have to be kidding. I saw the prices on that menu."

"You let me worry about those prices. It'll be my Christmas treat. That is, unless you forget all about me by Christmas."

"How could I forget the man who brought me to this wonderful place? But maybe you'll forget all about me."

"Not a chance! It's not every day a man meets a woman who's not only attractive but nice and fun to be with." As the boat came to a slow stop, Ted took Sammy's hand and assisted her up onto the dock. "In fact, I'm off again tomorrow. How about dinner again tomorrow night?"

I can't keep up this charade. I like this man, and he seems to like me. He deserves to know the truth. Well, at least part of it. "Ted," she began slowly, wishing she didn't feel compelled to be honest with him, "I'd love to have dinner with you tomorrow night, but the only dinner we can have together is if you want to come to my apartment and"—the words caught in her throat—"and eat hot dogs with three rambunctious kids." There—she'd said it.

five

"Kids?" Ted let go of her hand as if it were suddenly on fire, his jaw dangling nearly to his collarbone. "I thought, I mean—you said you weren't married. I didn't know you had kids—maybe—" He wanted out of there—fast. A woman with kids usually meant an ex-husband was in the picture, and he surely didn't want to find himself in the middle of a nasty triangle.

Sammy grabbed hold of his arm. "They're not my children, Ted. They're my sister's."

He felt ashamed at the way he'd backed away from her when she'd dropped what he thought was a bombshell. "Your sister's kids? She lives with you?"

Sammy shrugged. "No, she left her three children with me four years ago and took off with her boyfriend on his motorcycle. I have no idea when, or if, she's ever coming back. Meantime, her children are living with me."

"What a rotten thing to do." He shook his head. "Didn't she realize you have a life, too?"

"Oh, I don't mind. I love my nieces and nephew, but I'm not the one who should be raising them. They need their mother. I keep pictures of her around my apartment, and we talk about her a lot."

"Where were the kids tonight—when I picked you up?"

She gave him a sheepish grin. "Across the hall at my neighbor's. She's babysitting them. I should be getting back

70

soon. She has an early day tomorrow."

Three kids? He hadn't realized she had children in her life. "Ah, yeah, sure. You wait by the door while I go get the truck."

During his walk across the parking lot, Ted evaluated the situation. In some ways, Sammy having three children in her life was a definite turnoff. In other ways, her taking care of her sister's children made her even more attractive. Only an unselfish, loving woman would want to care for three young children who weren't hers. Surely they wouldn't be with her forever.

What if he fell in love with this woman and she ended up keeping those children until they were grown? Was he prepared to be a father—to someone else's children?

Ted shook his head then sucked in a deep breath of the night air. *Hey, man, what are you thinking? You met this attractive woman on a boat, took her to lunch, and now you two have had dinner together. That's not exactly a long-term commitment. Why don't you let life see where it leads you? Get to know her better and then decide how far you want this relationship to go. At this point, nothing is carved in stone. You might even like those kids.*

"I'm sorry, Ted," Sammy told him as she crawled into the front seat and reached for the seat belt. "I should have told you up front about the children."

He gazed at her pretty face. He liked her. He honestly liked her. This was the kind of woman he'd thought he'd never find—yet here she was. "Don't worry about it, Sammy. I think it's admirable of you to take on those children as you have. If the invitation still stands, I'd love to have hot dogs with all of you tomorrow night."

"You would? You're sure?" The surprised look on her face

nearly made him laugh.

"I'm sure. I'll bring the ice cream. All kids like ice cream. What's their favorite? Chocolate? Strawberry? Chocolate chip?"

"They love chocolate chip, but you really don't—"

"I want to, Sammy. If I didn't, I'd say so. What time?" The smile she gave him made it worthwhile.

"Seven?"

"Seven it is."

&

At exactly seven o'clock the next evening, Ted knocked on the door, two ice cream cartons in hand. But it wasn't Sammy who opened the door.

Before Ted knew what happened, someone tackled him about his waist, nearly bringing him to the floor, but fortunately he was able to grab hold of the doorframe and catch his balance.

"Simon! Stop! Let go of him!" Sammy moved to tug the young boy off Ted's legs. "I'm so sorry, Ted. Simon has more energy than he knows what to do with."

Stunned by what had just happened, Ted found himself speechless.

"Are you okay?"

"Uh, yeah, I guess so."

Taking hold of the boy's arm, Sammy lowered herself to his level. "Ted is our guest, Simon. You had no business tackling him like that."

The boy frowned. "I was only playing."

"That may be true, but you don't play that way with company, and Ted is our company. Tell him you're sorry."

"Why? I didn't hurt him."

"That may be true, but you could have hurt him. Apologize, Simon. Please."

Simon frowned and lowered his lip. "Don't want to."

Sammy sent Ted a look of embarrassment. "Then please go to your room. We need to talk about this in private."

"It's okay, really. Boys will be boys." Ted felt almost sorry for the boy. "No harm done." He bent and picked up the two cartons of ice cream from the floor. "Except for a little damage to the boxes. Someone from the Tennessee Titans ought to sign up that boy." *And maybe I should just cut and run. I'm not at all sure I'm up to this.*

"Please forgive Simon, Ted. I guess he was more excited about your coming than I realized, but that doesn't excuse his actions. I'd planned to greet you at the door with all three children lined up on the sofa, faces scrubbed until they shone, their hands folded in their laps, with gigantic smiles on their lips. Looks like my plan failed."

For the first time since arriving, Ted took a good look at his hostess. Sammy, in her pink knit shirt and jeans, looked fabulous. He wished he could sweep her up in his arms and carry her off somewhere, away from the responsibility of taking care of her sister's children.

"You look great," he finally mumbled, in awe of her wholesome beauty. She wasn't like the other women he'd met. They'd been—plastic. Not at all real, and out to impress him. Sammy was—Sammy. Nothing more. She seemed genuine to the core.

She smoothed a lock of hair that had fallen onto her forehead. "I don't feel great. Not after the welcome we gave you."

"Can we come in now?"

Ted turned to find two little girls peeking around the corner.

"Yes, you may come in." Sammy hurried toward them, taking each one by the hand and bringing them to stand before him.

"You've already met Simon. This," she said, pulling one of the girls forward, "is my sweet Tina. She's six."

Tina dipped her knee in a slight curtsey.

Ted reached out, took her small hand in his, and gave her a smile. "Hello, Tina. It's nice to meet you. You're a pretty little thing. You look a lot like your aunt."

"And this is Harley. She's nearly four and a half."

Harley wrapped her arm around Sammy's leg and clung to her, burying her face in her jeans.

Sammy stroked the young girl's silky blond hair. "Sometimes she's bashful, but she'll warm up to you when she gets to know you."

Ted felt as awkward as a blindfolded tightrope walker on a poorly stretched wire. He'd rarely been around children, except for his brother's kids. "Hi, Harley. I'll bet you like ice cream. I brought you some."

"She loves ice cream," Tina volunteered, speaking up for the first time since she'd entered the room.

Sammy took the cartons from his hands. "I'll put these in the freezer, and then, if you'll excuse me for a few minutes, I need to have a talk with Simon."

When he felt a tug on his pant leg, he looked down into Harley's big blue eyes.

"Would you read me a story?"

"Uh—why don't we wait for your aunt? She'll be right back."

"Aunt Sammy told you not to ask." Tina took hold of her sister's hand and led her to the sofa, helped her up, and then sat down beside her.

"But I want him to read me a story."

Ted appraised the situation and decided, even though he'd never read a story to a little girl before, he could probably manage it. "Where are your books?"

Tina gestured toward a magazine rack at the end of the sofa. Ted scanned the selection, finally pulling out a book about a fireman then seating himself beside Harley.

Before he could stop her, the little girl climbed onto his lap, wiggling around until she was comfortable. "Did you know I'm a fireman?" He opened the book and pointed to the picture on the first page. "Like him. I wear a uniform just like that."

Tina tugged on his sleeve. "Is it fun to be a fireman?"

Ted quirked up his face. "Most of the time. I like helping people and making sure they're safe."

She frowned. "I don't like the sirens. They scare me and make my ears hurt."

He couldn't help but laugh. "Sometimes they make my ears hurt, too."

Harley gave him a nudge with her elbow. "Read, please."

"Yes, ma'am." Ted opened the book and began to read. "Fireman Tom works at fire station number 5. He wears a blue shirt and blue pants. But when the alarm sounds, he hurries to the fire truck, slides his feet into his boots and then pulls on his big fireman coat, hat, and gloves before climbing onto the truck."

Tina scooted closer to him. "Firemen are nice. Simon said

they came to our house and put out a fire when our mother dropped her cigarette in our couch."

Ted shuddered at the thought of what could have happened to those children through their mother's carelessness. He'd seen it happen before. "I'm glad the firemen got there in time," he said, shaking his head before turning his attention back to the book.

"As you've found out, the children love to be read to." Sammy sat down in a chair opposite them. "The book you're holding is one of their favorites."

Looking up from the book, Ted could tell Sammy was upset. "You okay?"

She nodded. "Just a little frustrated with Simon. I don't know what's happening to him. He seems to get mouthier every day. I've taken away his TV time, cut off his allowance, and quit letting his friends come to visit, but I'm running out of options."

"I wish there was some way I could help." *Did I say that?*

"Thanks, but there's nothing you can do."

Harley nudged Ted again. "Read, please."

"No more reading, young lady. It's time to cook our hot dogs. I imagine Ted is hungry." Sammy pulled Harley from Ted's lap and straddled the child's legs over her hip before using her free hand to latch onto Tina's arm.

"Want me to go talk to Simon?"

Sammy gave Ted an incredulous look. "You want to?"

"Sure. I might not be able to accomplish anything, but I could try."

She nodded toward the hallway. "Go ahead. Just don't expect too much."

Squaring his shoulders and lifting his chin, he sent her a

guarded smile then moved toward the closed door. "Simon, can I come in?"

No answer.

"I thought we could talk. Man-to-man."

Still no answer.

"Go on in," Sammy called out from the living room. "There's no lock on the door."

After sucking in a deep breath, Ted turned the knob and stepped into the semidarkened room. "Did you pull down the shades like that? It's kinda dark in here." Ted moved toward the boy who was sitting on the side of the bed, his arms crossed defiantly over his chest, a deep scowl etched into his forehead. "I'd like to be your friend, Simon."

"Don't need any friends."

Using caution, ready for any kind of response, Ted lowered himself onto the bed beside the boy. "You like baseball?"

The boy's belligerent expression showed a slight softening. "Yeah, sorta."

"I loved baseball when I was your age. Ever been to a game? I mean a real game?"

Simon shook his head.

"My dad used to take me out to Greer Stadium when I was a kid. Bet you didn't know the Nashville Sounds are a triple-A farm team for the Milwaukee Brewers."

The boy gave him a blank stare.

"The Nashville Sounds are Nashville's home team. Boy, my dad and I've seen some really good games out at that stadium. You ever play T-ball?"

Simon shook his head again.

"Do you own a bat?"

Again the boy's head slowly rotated from side to side.

"How about a baseball?"

"Nope."

Ted searched his brain for something else to say. It appeared he was striking out with the baseball subject.

Simon's scowl lessened. "I had a ball once, but it got lost."

"You like to play catch?"

"I tried with my mom's boyfriend when I was little, but he got mad at me when I threw the ball over his head so I quit."

He scooted a bit closer to the boy. "Tell you what. Next time I come over I'll bring my ball, and you and I can play catch."

Sad eyes stared back. "No, don't want to."

"Why? It'll be fun."

"You'll get mad at me."

"No, I promise I won't. I remember how awful I was when I first started playing catch with my dad." He gave the boy a grin. "Once I hit him right between the eyes."

"Did he yell at you and call you names?"

"No, he didn't yell at me. He laughed." Ted slipped his arm around Simon's shoulders. "He knew I didn't mean to do it. You know what he did? He put his strong hand around mine and showed me how to grip the ball and throw it so it would go where I wanted it to. With a little practice, I got pretty good at it."

"I don't have a dad."

"You don't have to have a dad. All you need is a friend who is willing to show you how to do it. I'd like to be your friend, Simon. I still have the ball glove my dad gave me for my seventh birthday. It should fit you just fine. Want me to bring it over and teach you how to hold the ball and throw it?"

Simon's piercing eyes zeroed in on Ted. "Aren't you mad at me?"

"Mad at you?" Ted let out a chuckle. "For tackling me? No, I'm not mad, but I do have to admit I was a little surprised when you did it. You caught me off guard."

"I didn't mean to hurt you."

He tousled the boy's hair. "I knew you didn't. Why don't we forget about it and go help your aunt fix those hot dogs?" Ted rose. "I don't know about you, but I'm starved."

A slight smile curved at the corners of the boy's mouth as he stood and walked toward the door. "Me, too."

Not a victory but a good first start. Ted followed Simon into the kitchen and through the sliding glass door to where Sammy and the girls were setting the table on the patio outside her apartment.

Sammy looked up as they joined them. "Everything okay?"

Ted gave her a wink. "Yeah, Simon and I had a good talk. I think we're going to be good friends."

Sammy mouthed the word "thanks" then added aloud, "I hope you don't mind hot dogs cooked on the electric grill. I don't have an outdoor cooker."

Ted nodded toward her nephew. "We men are hungry. We like hot dogs cooked any old way, don't we, Simon?"

&

She couldn't believe it. Simon was actually smiling! "The hot dogs are nearly ready. Why don't you sit there, Ted, next to Simon, and I'll sit between the girls."

When they were seated, Sammy bowed her head and thanked the Lord for their food and asked Him to take care of the children's mother.

"Our mother is off riding on her boyfriend's motorcycle," Simon explained as he smeared mustard on his hot dog. "Do you have a motorcycle, Ted?"

"Nope, but I ride my friend's occasionally. I'm more into trucks. Maybe I can take you for a ride in mine sometime, if your aunt doesn't mind. I think you'll like it. It's got those shiny hubcaps that keep spinning even after my truck has stopped moving."

"I saw those on TV once. They're neat. Can I go, Aunt Sammy?"

Sammy continued to stare at Simon in amazement. He was not only smiling but also carrying on a conversation with Ted. "If Ted wants to take you, it's fine with me."

"And he's gonna show me how to throw a ball. He said he wouldn't even get mad if I threw it over his head."

She shot a grateful glance toward their guest. "That's really nice of Ted."

Ted winked at her. "Hey, every boy should know how to throw a ball. Simon and I might even take in a game out at Greer Stadium sometime."

"Ted and his daddy used to go to games there," Simon related with authority. "His dad taught him how to throw a ball like he's gonna teach me."

The five enjoyed their dinner as Ted related story after story about his own childhood. He was such a nice man, good-looking and apparently a good worker. He'd been at the fire department for a number of years and seemed to love it. It was hard to believe some woman hadn't snatched him up before now. Other than having trouble understanding God's will for something that happened in his life, was there another flaw she was missing? A hot temper maybe? No, if he'd had a hot temper or a short fuse, he would have exploded when Simon tackled him at the front door.

"What're you thinking about?" Ted nudged her elbow as he reached for the last hot dog on the plate.

"Just—things. Sorry. My mind wandered for a minute. It looks like the girls are finished. Maybe I'd better dip the ice cream."

He grabbed her arm as she stood. "I don't know how you do it, Sammy. Work a full-time job during the day and take care of these children nights and weekends. Don't you ever have time for just plain fun?"

"She plays games with us," Tina volunteered. "That's fun."

Ted let out a good-natured snort. "That wasn't exactly the kind of fun I meant, but knowing your aunt, I'm sure she enjoys playing games with you."

&

After the ice cream had been eaten, Sammy sent the girls into the living room to watch the video she'd rented for them and Simon to play with his handheld video game while she and Ted carried things back into the kitchen. "I've never seen Simon so agreeable," she told him, pulling open the refrigerator door and placing the mustard and catsup bottles on the shelf.

"It seems to me he has every right to be disagreeable. Oh, you're a great substitute mother, and I'm sure he enjoys living with you, but everyone knows a child longs for that perfect home and family."

"I wish these children had that perfect home and the love they deserve."

Ted moved toward her and encircled her in his arms. She smelled good. Like flowers. "They love you. I can tell."

Sammy's eyes widened. "And I love them. What I do for them, I do willingly and count it a privilege."

He responded with a sigh, in awe of her dedication.

"How much longer is your brother's family going to be with you?"

Ted shrugged his shoulders. "As long as they need to stay, I guess."

"I'm sure they appreciate your willingness to take them in as you have."

"Yeah, I guess they do, but I wish they'd show their appreciation by doing a better job with their kids. Those boys need the same kind of loving discipline you're giving Simon." Ted backed away then glanced at his watch. "Guess I'd better be going. I don't want to overstay my welcome. Besides, I have to work tomorrow."

"I do need to get the children bathed and to bed."

He hated to see the evening come to an end. "I've got an idea. They're having a Christian concert at the old Ryman Auditorium next weekend. I heard them advertise it on my car radio. I'm off Saturday. I'd like to take you." He was disappointed when she shook her head.

"Thanks for the invitation, but I can't go. My mom works every other Saturday and is dead tired when she gets home. I couldn't think of asking her to babysit after such a long day."

"What about your neighbor?"

"Saturday night is her bingo night. She plays every Saturday."

"Then we'll take the kids with us." *Did those words come out of my mouth?*

Sammy nodded toward the living room. "I—I don't know, Ted. They behave well in church." She chuckled. "Most of the time anyway—but a concert? I wouldn't want to embarrass you."

"If they get bored, we'll leave." He grabbed her hand. "Come on, Sammy. Say yes."

"Ted, you're such a nice man, and I appreciate your offer, but you really don't have to do this."

He tightened his grip on her hand. "Have to? I want to. I'm sure the kids'll do fine. The concert starts at eight, so I'll pick you up about seven, okay?" He loved it when her face brightened.

"If you're sure—"

"I'm sure." Bending, he planted a quick kiss on her cheek and released her hand. "Thanks for the great supper."

"Great supper? Hot dogs?"

"The hot dogs were good, but it was the company that made it special." He reached out his hand and was pleased when she took it. "I'll tell the kids good-bye and be on my way."

The pair walked into the living room where two sleepy-looking little girls huddled together in the corner of the sofa, their brother sitting on the other end, his full attention focused on the video game in his hand.

" 'Bye, Tina. 'Bye, Harley." Ted leaned over them and gently wiggled his fingers through their silky curls then reached out his hand toward Simon, who looked at it as if he wasn't exactly sure what he was supposed to do. Reaching his hand out even farther, Ted said, "Put it there, pal."

Simon grinned then grabbed Ted's hand and gave it a vigorous shake. " 'Bye, Ted."

Ted was happy when Sammy walked him to the door. He

wanted to kiss her good night, but this was only their second date, so maybe he'd be overstepping his mark. In fact, it wasn't even a date. She'd simply invited him over for dinner. "See you Saturday, about seven." The smile she gave him made him want to kiss her even more.

"I'll understand if you change your mind."

"No way, and you can't change your mind either, okay?" To his surprise she stood on tiptoe and kissed him on the cheek.

"Okay."

He backed awkwardly out the door. *Wow, what a woman!*

èa

"Hey, Benay, what's up with you?" Captain Grey sat down at the table next to Ted, coffee cup in hand. "You've been spacey ever since you came to work this morning."

"Spacey? Me?"

The captain nudged him with his elbow. "Yeah, you, Mr. Confirmed Bachelor. Anything happening between you and that little gal you met on the *General Jackson*?"

"I had hot dogs with her and her sister's three kids."

Jake sat down on the other side of Ted, his coffee cup coming down with a *kerplunk* on the table. "Hot dogs? That's it?"

Ted nodded, grinning. "Yeah, but we have another date next weekend."

Cal, who'd been listening but hadn't added to the conversation, leaned back in his chair, a smirk on his face. "A real date? Sure you can handle that? You aren't going to take those kids along, are you?"

Ted flinched. "Actually, yes. She doesn't have a babysitter for them."

Jake sputtered and nearly choked on his big swig of coffee.

"Babysitter? What about the kids' mother?"

"She ran out on them. Went off with some bozo on his motorcycle."

Cal shook his head. "Kinda hard to romance a gal with three kids."

Jake grabbed a doughnut from the sack in the middle of the table, broke off a chunk, and stuffed it into his mouth. "Hey, couldn't you find you some nice girl without kids?"

Cal nodded in agreement. "Kids can sure complicate things. Ask me. I married a woman with two of them. Between their needs and her ex-husband buttin' in where he's not wanted, life can be pretty miserable."

Captain Grey rose and placed his hand on Ted's shoulder. "Back off, guys. Give him a break. You've been bugging Ted for months to get himself a girlfriend. Now he has one."

As the fire alarm sounded throughout the station, drawing every man's immediate attention, Ted breathed a sigh of relief. He hated talking about himself and wondered why he'd even mentioned his upcoming date. He should have realized they'd make a big deal of it. Well, he wouldn't have to worry about that now. Duty called.

ᕽ

"Let me come over there and take care of the children Saturday night. I love spending time with them," Sammy's mother said when Sammy phoned her the next morning and told her about Ted's visit and his invitation. "I feel bad I can't help you out more with them."

"No, Mom, I can't ask you to do that. Besides, Ted wants them to go with us." Sammy smiled. "He's terrific, Mom. I've never met anyone like him. Even Simon likes him. But don't worry about the children. They'll be fine. I'm sure Ted wouldn't have invited them if he hadn't wanted them."

"Maybe it's you he wants, dear. Did you ever think of that? A man willing to invite three children along on a date must want to spend time with you."

Sammy glanced at her image in the mirror and adjusting her neckline. "I haven't told him about my—surgery."

"You've only had a few dates, sweetie. I doubt he's told you everything about himself. Maybe he has athlete's foot. Don't worry about it. If things develop between you, you can tell him then. Meanwhile, just enjoy yourself."

Sammy snickered at her mother's choice of words. "Athlete's foot is hardly the same as having someone else's heart beating in your chest."

"Everything in its time, sweetheart. Do what you think best, but if I were in your place, I'd wait and tell him later, when the two of you know one another better."

"What you're saying is, don't scare him off any sooner than necessary, right?"

"I guess you could say that. Ever hear the phrase 'don't borrow trouble'? Telling him now may be pointless. At this stage in your relationship, you two barely know one another."

"You're probably right, but I don't want you worrying about us. We're definitely taking the children along. You spend the evening with Dad. With his physical problems, he needs you more than we do. Give him a big kiss and hug for me, okay?"

"Okay, but if you change your mind, I'm more than happy to keep the children for you."

"I won't change my mind, but thanks for the offer. Talk to you later, Mom."

Sammy thought over her mother's words. Maybe she was being needlessly concerned. Who knew? Their Saturday date could be their last one. Maybe he'd never invite her out again. Why go into detail about something unnecessary? She'd wait and see what the weekend held before deciding when she should tell him.

She was tempted to buy a new outfit for the concert but decided she had plenty of appropriate things hanging in her closet. Besides, shopping with three children was hardly worth it. After trying on at least six outfits, she selected her navy blazer and off-white skirt, topped with a lightweight red turtleneck shirt.

By the time the doorbell rang the following Saturday night, she was a bundle of nerves. Harley had resisted taking a much-needed nap, Tina spilled orange juice on her best dress and had to change it at the last minute, and Sammy couldn't locate one of the earrings she'd wanted to wear. To her amazement, the only person who seemed in control was Simon, and he'd been dressed and playing with his video game for over an hour.

"Wow, you look beautiful," Ted told her when she pasted on a smile and opened the door with little Harley in her arms and Tina by her side.

Before she could respond with a thank-you, Simon shot past her, his hand extended. "Hi, Ted."

"Well, hi, yourself, Simon." Ted gave his hand a vigorous shake then reached out a ball glove. "Didn't think I'd remember, did you?"

The boy's eyes shone. "This is the one your dad gave you?"

Ted bobbed his head. "Sure is. I thought you could keep it

here, and next time I come over we'll play catch. That okay with you?"

"Yeah." Simon took the glove and slipped it onto his hand. "Hey, look! It fits!"

Ted grinned. "I told you it would. Take good care of it, okay?"

"Maybe you shouldn't—"

Ted put his finger to Sammy's lips. "Don't worry about it. If I hadn't wanted Simon to have it, I wouldn't have brought it. Everybody ready to go? We're going to have to ride in my truck, but it has an extended cab so there should be room for everyone."

After carefully placing the glove on the sofa, Simon raced to the door. "Your truck. Wow. Now I can see your hubcaps."

"You have to sit quietly," Sammy told the children later as the usher led the five to their seats in the big historic auditorium.

"I want a drink."

All eyes turned toward Harley. Sammy gave her niece a slight frown. "Not now, baby. You had a drink just before you left home."

Ted smiled at the little girl. "Maybe we can get something to drink after the concert."

"I want one now."

Sammy brushed a lock of hair from Harley's forehead. "No, Harley. Not until after the concert is over." She gestured toward the stage. "In a minute those curtains will open and—"

"I need a drink, too."

With a frown, Sammy turned toward Tina who was sitting on the other side of her. "You and your sister are going to have to wait. I warned you before we left home that—"

"Want me to take them?"

Her frown disappearing, Sammy smiled. "No. Thank you, Ted, but it's important that I follow through when I've told the children something. Don't worry about them. I doubt they'll go into dehydration before the concert ends." She'd barely gotten the words out when the lights dimmed, the curtains opened, and the concert began. Sammy glanced from child to child, each one's attention focused on the sight and the sounds of the music. Then she looked at Ted, who smiled at her approvingly and gave her a thumbs-up. But by the time an intermission was announced, all three children, especially young Harley, were getting fidgety.

"I have to go to the bathroom," Simon announced the moment the auditorium lights came on.

২৬

Ted leaned toward Sammy. "Why don't I take him?"

"If you don't mind, that'd be great. That way I can take the girls to the ladies' room and then get them a drink."

"Sounds good to me. We'll meet you back here." He stepped out into the aisle, making way for Sammy and the girls to pass, then motioned toward the boy. "Come on, Simon. We'd better hurry if we don't want to stand in a long line."

Apparently it was too late. The line extended into the hallway. Just as they were about to enter the men's restroom, another man exited, a former classmate of Ted's. "Brian! Long time no see."

"Hey, Ted. Where've you been keeping yourself?"

"You go on, Simon," Ted told the boy as he reached out to shake his friend's hand. "I'll wait for you out here." He watched until Simon disappeared inside then moved to join his friend.

"That your kid?" Brian asked, nodding toward the doorway.

Ted laughed. "Nope, 'fraid not. Simon's the nephew of a friend of mine. How about you? You got kids?"

"Yep, three of them. I heard you were a fireman. That true?"

For the next several minutes the men conversed, laughing and catching up on the more than eight years since they'd seen one another. Ted noted the crowd around them was thinning out. "Well, I'd better go find Simon so we can get back to our seats. Good to see you, Brian."

"Yeah, good to see you, too."

Ted walked into the men's room, which was nearly deserted, but Simon was nowhere in sight. "Simon," he called out, stooping to check beneath the stall doors. "You in here?"

No answer.

His heart racing, he rushed out into the hall. "Simon?" But Simon wasn't there either. *He probably went back to his seat*, Ted reasoned, as he made his way to their section. But as he reached their aisle the lights dimmed, and the second half of the concert started. Narrowing his eyes, he finally located their seats. There sat Sammy and the two girls, but no Simon. His heart pounded in his ears. *Where could Simon be?*

He hurried back out into the hall, retracing his footsteps to the men's room. Still no Simon. Should he go back and tell Sammy he'd lost the boy? Contact security? Surely the theater had some kind of security set up. *I don't have kids! I have no idea what to do!*

"Are you having trouble locating your seat, sir?"

Ted spun around and found a lady wearing a badge with

the word USHER printed on it staring at him. "No, I've lost someone, a nine-year-old boy."

"Was he wearing a red sweater?"

Ted nodded. "Yes, have you seen him?"

She placed a consoling hand on Ted's arm and smiled at him. "Yes, he couldn't remember where he was sitting, so I walked him up and down the aisles until we located his aunt. He's in his seat."

"Whew! You have no idea how relieved I am. I was so afraid something had—"

"He's fine. Nice little boy. He even thanked me for helping him."

"And I thank you, too. Guess I'd better get back to my seat before they send out a posse to find me."

Sammy leaned across Simon and touched Ted's wrist as he sat down. "Where were you? I was beginning to worry when Simon said he couldn't find you."

"*He* couldn't find *me*?" Deciding it wouldn't be polite to carry on a conversation and disturb those seated around them, he shrugged and whispered, "I'll tell you later."

By the time the concert ended, Harley was sound asleep in Ted's arms with the sleeping Tina curled up in Sammy's lap. Ted had to laugh to himself as he gazed at his little group. To anyone who didn't know them, they probably looked like the average American family. Mom, Dad, and three kids. All they needed was a minivan, a dog, and a house with a white picket fence. And though those things had scared him in the past, somehow now they didn't seem half bad.

"We had a great time, Ted," Sammy told him once she'd tucked the children in bed.

After one final glance at the eleven o'clock news, he hit the off button on the remote, leaned back against the sofa, and motioned her to sit beside him. "I had a great time, too."

"You never did tell me how you lost Simon."

Ted sucked in a deep breath and circled his arm across the sofa's back. "I didn't lose him. I was waiting for him in the hall right outside the restroom door, visiting with an old school friend. He managed to get past me without my seeing him."

Smiling, she leaned back into his arm. "No harm done. That nice usher helped him find me, but I started to worry when Simon said he couldn't find you."

"Guess he just missed me in the crowd. I really felt bad." Ted gave her a hesitant grin. "Actually I panicked. Here you'd entrusted him into my care, and I'd let him get away. I was so afraid something had happened to him."

"Well, it didn't. Take it from me. Simon has a propensity for wandering off. I have to keep my eye on him. He's curious about everything."

Ted tightened his arm around her shoulders, enjoying the delicate scent of her hair. "You sure you're not saying that to make me feel better?" What was it about her that drew him to her? He'd dated other women, without the family entanglements she had; yet he hadn't felt the same vibes with them as he did when he was with her.

Tilting her head slightly, she smiled at him. "No, it's the truth. He's always wandering off. I don't think he does it on purpose. As I said, he's just curious, and his curiosity gets him into trouble."

For a moment Ted stared into her beautiful eyes, eyes that reminded him of a Tennessee sky on a cloudless day. "I was kinda like that myself when I was a kid. I was fascinated by anything that worked, made a sound, or took batteries. I had to know what made them tick."

"Guess it's a man thing." Sammy tugged her collar up about her neck.

"You cold?" Ted used his question as an excuse to pull her even closer.

"No, I'm fine. Are you cold?"

"No, just right. What are your plans for tomorrow?"

Sammy's brow creased. "Tomorrow?"

"Yeah, I'm off again tomorrow. I thought maybe we could do something together."

She turned to face him with a look of surprise. "Are you serious? I thought after spending the evening with three rowdy kids, you'd want to run for the door and I'd never see you again."

He huffed. "It wasn't so bad, although I admit Simon disappearing gave me a few anxious moments. The kids were much better behaved than I thought they'd be. My nephews could learn a lot from them."

A smile returned to her face. "Back to your question. Since tomorrow is Sunday, the kids and I will be going to church, but you could come along."

"I usually drive to where my parents lives and go to my home church with them."

"Maybe they wouldn't mind if you missed this one time." Sammy took his free hand and folded it in hers. "We'd like for you to come with us."

How could he refuse that beautiful face? The pleading of those big blue eyes?

"The children are in Sunday school during the worship service, and my substitute is filling in for me and teaching my class, so it'll be just the two of us."

"Just the two of us? You mean I can have you all to myself for one whole hour?"

She gave him a childish giggle that set his heart singing.

"Maybe longer. I might be able to persuade my mom to take them home with her, and we could have the afternoon to ourselves. That is, if you *want* to spend the afternoon with me."

"You drive a hard bargain."

"Only because I enjoy your company." Sammy glanced at the clock. "I hate to say it, but I think we'd better call it a night. I need to get to bed. I'll have to be up by six to get my shower and make sure the children are bathed, fed, and dressed in time." She stood and reached out her hand.

He took it, stood, then slipped his arm around her waist and guided her toward the door. "Makes me tired thinking about all the work you have to do just to get to church."

"So are you coming with me?" she asked, pulling the door open before gazing into his eyes.

After wrapping her in his arms, Ted grinned down at Sammy. "On one condition."

She eyed him warily. "Condition? What condition?"

"That you let me kiss you good night."

❧

Sammy's heart did a cartwheel. She'd longed for Ted's kiss since the day he'd shown up at her office, but she'd never expected it to happen. Now here she was, being held in his arms, and he was asking to kiss her. Not only that, their kiss was the condition that would bring Ted to her church. He had to be joking.

"What's your answer, Sammy?" he whispered, his chin nuzzling her hair as he drew her nearer to him. "Are you going to let me kiss you good night?"

She sent him a timid smile. "I do want you to go to church with me, Ted, but I can't trade you a kiss for it. It wouldn't be right."

"Does that mean I can kiss you whether I go to church with you or not?"

Her smile widened. "That's not exactly what I said."

Using his forefinger to tilt her face upward, Ted slowly leaned toward her until his lips brushed hers.

The touch of his lips, the scent of his aftershave, the tender way his arms held her close, made her almost giddy. She held her breath, hoping just by holding it, her throbbing heart would settle down.

Though Sammy tried to hold back, she thought she would explode with joy as his lips pressed against hers and she was enfolded in his strong arms, his fingers splayed across her back. Their kiss was pure ecstasy. When it finally ended, she leaned into him, reveling in the moment, one she would treasure forever.

Slowly Ted released her, his gaze locking with hers as they parted. "What time should I pick you up?" he asked, seeming as dazed as she felt.

"Ten," she answered weakly, not even sure her words were loud enough to be heard.

"Ten it is." He started to step out the door but stopped, gazing at her with eyes that told her their kiss had been special to him, too. "One for the road?"

Feeling more feminine than she had in a long time, Sammy

gave him a demure smile, then stood on tiptoe and kissed his cheek.

"Nice, but not exactly what I had in mind." Wrapping his arms about her again, his lips sought hers, and his kiss made her head spin. "Good night. Thanks for a great evening."

Dipping her head to avoid his gaze, Sammy backed away, her legs trembling and threatening to crumple beneath her. "Good night, Ted."

After gazing at her for a few more seconds, he stepped outside, closing the door behind him. Sammy turned and leaned against it, her fingers gently touching her lips, as if by touching them she could preserve the kisses he'd bestowed upon them.

Her moment of overwhelming joy collapsed as her hand went to her heart. *I have to tell him. Soon. Though our attraction for each other may never go beyond where it is now, it's not fair to keep something like this from him. It seems that, just by being my friend, he has the right to know the heart beating within me is not my own.*

Her mother's words came racing back. *Don't borrow trouble. Telling him at this early stage of your relationship may be pointless.*

"You may be right, Mom," Sammy said aloud, glancing at her mother's photograph on the mantel. "The last thing I'd want, though, would be to hurt Ted by keeping the truth from him. But I can't take the chance of having him turn away now, especially since he's agreed to go to church with me. The truth will have to wait a little longer."

≈

Ted crawled into his truck and turned the key in the ignition, visions of the lovely Sammy rotating through his mind. She was the kind of woman he'd hoped to find one day, and he'd just kissed her. Giving his head a wake-up shake, his hands came thudding down on the steering wheel. *Man, what are you thinking? She may be everything you ever wanted, but what about those kids? From the sound of it, that sister of hers may never come back. Do you want to be saddled with three kids who aren't even yours? Especially when you'd almost decided you don't even want children?*

He shifted into drive and nudged the truck slowly forward. *Who knows? Maybe her sister will come back. I can't let her guardianship of those children stand between me and the first woman I've been truly interested in. I think I'll hang around for a while at least and see what happens.*

❧

Sammy was up a full thirty minutes before her alarm sounded, despite the fact that thinking about the unexpected kiss had kept her awake half the night. Nonetheless, she was excited about the day that was about to unfold before her—until she showered and caught a glimpse of her image in the mirror. Though most of the redness had long since faded, to Sammy, the nasty scar was as ugly as ever. *But without this scar and what it represents, I'd no doubt be a dead woman by now.*

"Up, up, time to get up," she told Simon while rousting him out of bed an hour later. "Guess what! Ted is going to church with us!"

Simon, who was always the hardest to get out of bed, peeked out from under the covers. "He is?"

"Yes, and guess what else! I talked to Grandma, and she wants you guys to spend the afternoon with her and Grandpa. Isn't that great?"

Simon eyed her suspiciously. "Are you and Ted going to Grandma's, too?"

"No, I'm spending the afternoon with Ted."

Simon threw back the covers, sat up in bed, and crossed his arms over his chest. "I wanna stay with you and Ted. He promised he'd play catch with me."

Sammy reached for the boy's hand and tugged him to his feet. "And I'm sure he will. Just not today."

Pulling away from her grasp, Simon dropped back onto the bed, a scowl marring his face. "Then I'm not going to church."

Her first impulse was to order him out of bed and into the bathtub, but she remembered how he'd unexpectedly taken to Ted and smiled at him instead. "I'm sure Ted will play catch with you as soon as he gets time. You wouldn't want to disappoint Grandma and Grandpa, would you? They're looking forward to your visit. Now hurry up and get your bath. You *are* going to church."

She smiled as she said it but added a firmness to her voice, which she hoped would settle the matter. To her relief, Simon slid to his feet and padded quietly toward the bathroom.

While he bathed, Sammy awakened the two girls and gave them their breakfast. By nine thirty, all three children were lined up on the sofa, dressed in their Sunday best, waiting for Ted while Sammy hurriedly tidied up the kitchen.

The parking lot was nearly full by the time they arrived at the church. After delivering the children to their Sunday school classes, Sammy led him through the welcome center toward the sanctuary, stopping briefly along the way to introduce him to Pastor Day and other friends and acquaintances.

"Oh, look—there's my mom. I want you to meet her." Taking hold of his hand, she led him toward a group of women who were engaged in conversation. She touched her mother's elbow. "Mom, this is the man I've been telling you about. Ted Benay. Ted, this is my mom."

Ted extended his hand. "Hello, Mrs. Samuel. I've heard a lot about you, too."

Mrs. Samuel wrapped her arm about her daughter's shoulders and smiled. "It's nice to finally meet you, Ted, but don't believe everything this girl says. She's biased. By the way, Sammy, you needn't pick up the children this evening. Your father and I will drive them home."

"Are you sure? I know Dad doesn't like you driving after dark. I could come—"

"I'm sure. Besides, it's not that far. We'll plan to have them home about seven. You two have a great day and don't give the children a second thought. They'll be fine."

After thanking her mother, Sammy linked her arm in Ted's, and they stepped into the sanctuary.

"Nice church. It's much bigger than the one I go to," Ted admitted after he and Sammy were seated in a pew near the front. "God's probably looking down and saying, 'What's Ted Benay doing here? This isn't his home church.'"

Sammy gave him a playful nudge. "I'm sure He's glad you're in church, even if it isn't the one you usually attend."

"You think so?"

"I know so."

"I only came here today because I wanted to be with you."

"And I asked you because I wanted to be with you. I'm glad you're here."

The sound of the church's mighty organ filled the sanctuary as the organist began playing the prelude, temporarily ending their conversation. Sammy was delighted when Ted sang the hymns and worship choruses along with her and was surprised at the richness of his voice.

"You must have sung in the choir, right?" she asked him as they made their way through the double doors toward the parking lot when the service ended. "You have a great voice."

He nodded. "Yep, used to every Sunday. Even did a few solos, but since I work so many Sundays now, I'm not able to anymore. Though I don't go regularly, I still love the Lord. But I sure don't understand the way He does things."

"He never promised we'd understand. I know there are things in my life I don't understand, but I have to trust Him."

"It isn't that I don't trust Him—though maybe that's part of it. I just wish I understood Him."

She couldn't be sure, but she thought she heard a note of despair in his voice, a sadness. What could have happened to make him question God's will?

His demeanor suddenly changed to one of happiness, and he spun her around to face him. "Enough of this gloom and doom—where shall we eat lunch? They have a fabulous Sunday buffet at Martha's at the Plantation Restaurant on the grounds of the old Belle Meade mansion. Or we could go to Calhoun's and have their famous ribs. Or maybe to Mario's for Italian or the New Orleans Manor for seafood. Your choice. You name it."

Sammy's eyes widened. "Aren't those all a bit expensive?"

"Not when you're taking your best girl out to dinner."

Her breath caught in her throat. "Best girl?"

Ted winked then pulled open the door of his truck and, with a grand swoop of his arm, motioned her inside. "Best and only girl."

She moved past him, accepted his hand to assist her into the truck, and then winked back. "And you're my best and only guy. Today."

After closing her door he hurried around to the driver's side and crawled in. "Today? Does that mean you have another guy warming up in the wings to take over my spot tomorrow?"

Tilting her head coyly, she gave him a teasing smile. "That's for me to know and you to find out."

He twisted the key in the ignition, revved up the engine, and turned to face her, his expression serious as his hand went to the gearshift. "I wasn't joking, Sammy. You *are* my best girl. If you feel the same way about me, I'd like for us to spend time together and get to know each other better."

Stunned yet excited by his words, she gaped at him. "You really mean that?"

He smiled. "Wouldn't have said it if I didn't. Seems like all I do lately is think about you."

"I—" She lowered her head, her fingers working nervously at the mock turtleneck of her shirt. "I—think about you all the time, too."

His smile turned into a full-fledged grin, and he shoved the gearshift into drive then fell in line with the other vehicles waiting to exit the parking lot. "Now that that's settled, tell me where you want to eat and what you would like to do for the rest of the afternoon."

"Can we go anywhere I'd like? We don't need to go to such expensive places. My tastes are pretty simple."

"Believe me, price makes no difference, but, as I said, you name it. This is your day. We'll do whatever you want."

"Then I'd like to pick up a bucket of the Colonel's chicken, mashed potatoes, and slaw, rent a couple of movies, then kick off our shoes and eat a leisurely meal at my apartment."

Ted took his eyes off the traffic ahead of him long enough to eye her suspiciously. "You're kidding, right?"

She shook her head. "No, I'm absolutely serious. I can't remember when I last sat down to a meal at my house without having to jump up every few minutes to wipe up spilled milk, refill a plate, referee a spat, or take a child to the bathroom. Eating a meal at home today, without the patter of little feet, would be a real luxury. And watching a movie? An entire movie not designated for viewers under thirteen? I can't even remember the last one I saw in its entirety. It doesn't even need to be a chick flick. A comedy or an action movie would be fine. A treat indeed."

Ted maneuvered his truck out onto the street and into the line of traffic then reached across the seat and grabbed her hand, giving it a squeeze. "Lady, you are my kind of woman. A bucket of chicken and a couple of movies it is."

Sammy let out a sigh of satisfaction. "So I'm a cheap date. What can I say?" Her heart pounded furiously at the thought of spending the entire afternoon with him.

After nearly thirty minutes giggling over the movie selections and finding two they agreed on, they picked up the chicken. It was well after one o'clock when they entered her apartment. They'd scarcely closed the door when Ted's cell phone rang.

"Hello." He paused. "Yes, I have it. Why?"

The expression on Ted's face told Sammy not only was

something wrong, but Ted was upset about it. When he finally hung up he said, "It seems my nephews found my bowling ball in the back of the hall closet in a box under some magazines where I'd hidden it from them. They were rolling it across my living room floor and hit the sliding glass door leading onto my balcony and shattered it. That was my sister-in-law wanting to know if I had homeowner's insurance."

Sammy's eyes widened. "Was anyone hurt?"

"No. I thought sure I'd hidden it so they wouldn't find it. I probably should have locked it in the storage container in my truck bed, but that's hindsight."

Sammy watched as he put the phone back into its belt holster. "Do you have to go home and board up the opening?"

"Not now. It's nice outside. I'll do it later. I'm not about to let a little broken glass ruin our day. I told her where to find the phone number for my insurance company and to go ahead and call them. I hope she and my brother will clean up the mess. If not, I'll do it when I get home."

She smiled and patted the cushion next to her on the sofa. "Maybe some nice tender chicken will make you feel better." She reached into the carryout sack, pulled out its contents, and placed them on the coffee table in front of them. "If, after we pray, the chicken and the mashed potatoes have cooled off, I'll zap them in the microwave."

"Good. Those things are so much better hot." Ted accepted the plate then bowed his head and remained silent while she prayed, echoing her amen.

After their meal, he helped her clean up before they went back into the living room to watch their first movie.

"How about some popcorn?" she asked when the movie

ended and the credits began to roll.

"With lots of butter and salt?"

She wrinkled up her nose. "I guess this one time wouldn't clog up our arteries too much."

He followed her into the kitchen. "I hope I didn't sound grumpy earlier. You know, about the bowling ball."

"I thought you took the news fairly well." She pulled the popcorn bag from the cabinet, placed it in the microwave and hit the button marked POPCORN.

Ted rubbed at his temples. "Okay. We've talked a lot about me but very little about you. Tell me something about yourself, Sammy, something I don't already know."

He gave her a playful nudge. "Have you always been as perfect as you are now? Surely you have a few flaws."

Yes, one huge one running right down the center of my chest. "Perfect? That's the last word I would use to describe myself. I'm impatient with the children, put off my bill paying until the last minute, let my laundry go until the hamper is running over, hate to clean the bathroom, forget where I left my cell phone, drive my car until the gas peg is on empty—"

Ted laughed. "Those are the worst flaws you can think of? Sammy, those are nothing, not even worth mentioning. Come on—surely you can do better than that. Give me one big flaw."

She trembled at his question. *This is the perfect opportunity to tell him. Maybe I'd better just blurt it out and get it over with.*

The dinger sounded as the microwave shut off. Ted carefully lifted out the hot bag then rubbed his hands briskly together. "Mmm, hot popcorn. Looks like you're off the hook, momentarily anyway. Let's take this into the living room and eat it before it gets cold."

Sammy's body went limp. She felt like a prisoner getting a last-minute reprieve from the governor. "Ah, good idea."

"I know you have a brother. Do you have any other siblings?" She hoped to change the subject and avoid talking about herself once they were seated again on the sofa, sharing the popcorn directly from the opened bag.

He stopped eating, his hand poised in midair. "Why did you ask me that?"

Did his voice have a sharp edge to it, or was it her imagination? "I'm curious, that's all. You said we should get better acquainted."

A deep sigh seemed to come from the pit of his stomach as he stared at her. "Sorry, Sammy. I didn't mean to snap at you. In answer to your question, no, other than my brother I don't have any other siblings. Not now. Tiger—that's what I called my twin sister—died several years ago in a car accident. She never regained consciousness."

Startled by his revelation, she grabbed hold of his arm, nearly knocking the popcorn bag out of his hand. "Oh, Ted, I'm so sorry. She was your twin? That must have made her loss even harder."

Closing his eyelids tightly, he bit at his lip. "Tiger and I were close. I—I still can't believe she's gone. She was such a beautiful woman, inside and out."

Sammy slid closer and wrapped her arm around his neck, her head resting against his. She wanted so much to comfort him, but other than "I'm sorry" what could she say? "Is—is that why you question God's will? Because He took your sister?"

His misty eyes turned cold. "Wouldn't you question God if He took your sister in the prime of her life or one of those children you're caring for?"

"Without going through the experience I can't honestly say, but I don't think I'd *question* His will. I'd be upset at their loss and wonder *why* He took them, but God knows best. God created us. He has every right to take us when He chooses."

Ted pointed an accusing finger in her direction. "You're right about one thing. *You* can't say without going through the experience, but I can. I've been there. I've felt the horrible pain of losing someone I loved."

Her heart went out to him. "We've all lost someone we love. Maybe not a twin sister, but that doesn't mean we should blame God. We see only our side and the grief we feel. God sees the whole picture. It's never easy to lose a loved one under any circumstance, whether by old age, natural causes, illness, or an accident. Though losing someone that close to you, without a chance to tell them good-bye, has to be one of the worst horrors a human being can endure."

A visible tremor racked through Ted's body. "Especially if *you* were the one driving the car!"

A jolt of surprise raced through her body like a sudden electric shock. "*You* were driving the car?"

The pain of remembrance showed on his face. "Yeah, me. Her very own brother. I tried to stop in time when that fool's car came barreling through the intersection, but I couldn't. If only I'd sped up or slowed down or had been ten seconds earlier or ten seconds later, he wouldn't have hit us, and she might have—"

Placing her palms on his cheeks, Sammy swiveled his face toward hers. "Look at me. Listen to me. You can't blame yourself, Ted. It was the other person's fault. Not yours. Though I didn't have the privilege of knowing your sister, I'm sure she wouldn't have blamed you. You can't go on letting that accident eat you up like this."

Tears rolled down his cheeks. "She wasn't wearing her seat belt, and that was my fault, too. I'd asked her to get my sunglasses out of my jacket, which I'd left in the backseat. She'd taken off her seat belt to reach for them just before that car hit us. If she'd had it on, maybe she would have survived."

With her thumbs, Sammy gently brushed away his tears. "And maybe it wouldn't have made any difference. That's something you'll never know. You told me that even though you're questioning God, you still love Him. Surely you haven't forgotten the scripture that says all things work together for good to them that love God. I know it's hard to believe any good could come from your sister's death, but we can't second-guess God's will. From the sound of things, your life could have been taken, too. He spared *your* life. He must have a purpose for you."

"I understand that, and I'm thankful I'm alive. But why would He take my beautiful, talented sister and leave me behind? It didn't make sense." Ted pulled one of the paper napkins from the stack the store had given him when he'd picked up the chicken and wiped at his eyes. "Losing her was bad enough, but what the rest of my family agreed to do really upset me."

six

Sammy's eyes widened. Unless he was talking about his sister being cremated, which many people didn't want for their loved ones, she had no idea what he was talking about.

"They wanted her heart to be removed from her body and given to someone else!"

His words struck Sammy with such force, they nearly rendered her helpless. She felt sick to her stomach, as if she was going to throw up. Pushing away from him, she leaned back against the sofa, clutching its arm for support, struggling to catch her breath.

"I guess my sister had signed a donor card, but she hadn't told me about it." He was apparently so absorbed in telling about the accident that he hadn't noticed her reaction. "Can you imagine loving parents giving permission to do something like that to their daughter? I couldn't. I fought them on it, but I was overruled. They were for it, and Tiger had signed that card. I still haven't forgiven them for it. According to that card, she donated her eyes, liver, and other organs, too. They took them all. I still wish my sister had asked me before someone talked her into signing that stupid card."

"But—but—" Her borrowed heart pounded so loudly she could barely hear him. Sammy struggled for words, any words, but they wouldn't come. Finally she managed to say faintly, "But that heart—gave someone else life. Doesn't that make it worthwhile?"

He held up his hand to silence her. "Don't even try, Sammy. Believe me, I've heard all the arguments, and I still disagree. It's my opinion that if God wanted a person with a bad heart to live, He would heal them. I've heard heart recipients only live a few years anyway."

"But a few years could mean a world to the person who needed that heart."

"Losing my sister was the most devastating thing that ever happened to me, especially since I was driving the car, but the idea of having Tiger's heart beating in someone else's body was the crowning blow. If God wanted that other person to live, why didn't He just keep their heart from going bad?"

"I—I don't know."

"I hope I never meet the person who has her heart. I could never look them in the eye, knowing it took my sister's death to keep them alive."

"But, Ted, if your sister was a Christian, her spirit went to be with the Lord, leaving her body behind. That body was only the shell in which she lived."

"That may be true, but that body she left behind was the part of her that I, and everyone else who loved her, saw and loved, and I didn't want anything to happen to it."

For the first time since beginning his upsetting disclosure, Ted looked directly at Sammy. "Your cheeks are flushed. Aren't you feeling well?"

Tugging at her collar, she lowered her head, avoiding his penetrating gaze. "I do feel a little woozy."

He placed his flattened palm on her forehead and frowned. "You feel warm. Can I get you a drink of water?"

"I think I have a headache coming on." She slowly rotated her head from side to side, her fingertips massaging her temples. "Sometimes lying down helps."

"Do you want me to go?"

"No. Go ahead and watch the other movie. I just need to shut my eyes for a while." *And absorb what you said and decide if this is the time I should tell you about my heart or if I should wait until you're not already upset.*

He pushed a lock of hair from her forehead. "I hope my ranting and raving didn't cause your headache."

With great effort she lifted the corners of her mouth into a weak smile. "You only said what you felt. Your words helped me understand you better."

"I've never spelled it out like that to anyone except my family and the man from the mortuary. But with you I felt I could open up, that maybe you'd be the only one to understand my feelings."

I'm the last person who would understand your feelings!

He impatiently grabbed his cell phone when it rang again. Sammy watched him answer it, her insides still churning.

"A toothache, huh? That sounds pretty miserable." Ted's eyes darted toward her. "Yeah, I can come. You'd do the same for me. I'll be there in twenty minutes." He flipped the phone shut. "A buddy of mine, one of the firemen on B shift, has a doozy of a toothache. He wants me to come and finish out his shift for him. I hope you don't mind. I hated to tell him no."

Though it upset Sammy to see him leave so soon, in some ways she was relieved. "But aren't you working tomorrow?"

"Yeah. I keep some extra clothes and shaving gear in my locker at the station, so I'll be fine. But I hate to leave you, especially since you're not feeling well." Cupping her hands in his, he gave her a look of concern. "Take something for that headache, okay?"

"I will."

He glanced at his watch. "I'd better scoot. Can I call you later?"

She nodded. "Yes, that would be nice."

He said a quick good-bye then closed the door, leaving Sammy standing in the middle of the living room, her head throbbing, her heart pounding furiously, and her mind in a whirl.

"A lot of people feel that way about donating their loved one's organs, Sammy," her mother told her three hours later as they stood in Sammy's kitchen preparing mugs of hot cocoa for the children. "Literally thousands of people have signed donor cards and want their organs donated, but Ted's feelings are not that unusual. No one likes the idea of having their loved one's body desecrated." She shrugged. "Even knowing how important it is that someone donated their heart to you, if I lost your father I'd have trouble giving permission for the same reasons Ted has. Maybe I've watched too many of those reality shows on TV where they show parts of an autopsy. Even though I know it's staged, I couldn't bear the thought."

"Neither could I!" Sammy grabbed her mother's arm. "That's what makes me so thankful my donor and their family had the courage to do what they did. Otherwise I might not be here now."

"You must tell him, dear, now that he's poured out his heart to you. You know that, don't you? For his sake *and* for yours. I know I said earlier you should wait, but the time has come.

The longer you put it off, the harder it's going to be for both of you. He may not take the news as badly as you expect him to."

"Hey, what's taking so long?" Sammy's father called out from the living room. "These kids are clamoring for their cocoa."

"Be right there, Dad." Sammy circled her arm around her mother and gave her a loving squeeze. "Pray for me, Mom. I want to do the right thing, but it's so hard. I don't want to lose Ted."

"I will, sweetie. God has a plan for your life. If Ted is to be part of that plan, he will be."

Those words echoed over and over in Sammy's mind as she lay curled up beneath the quilt that night, waiting for sleep to overtake her. Finally, after burying her face in the pillow, she released the flood of tears she'd been working so hard to hold back. *Oh, Ted, what have I done? What have I done? If I'd been up-front with you at the beginning, I would never have fallen in love with you, and this wouldn't have happened. But I am in love with you, and I can't stand the thought of losing you. I'm so confused. Only God can get me out of the mess I've made!*

❧

Sammy stared aimlessly out her office window the next morning, sipping the cup of hot coffee she'd purchased from the vending machine in the hall, wondering what kind of night it had been at the fire station. Her phone rang once, twice, then a third time before she turned to answer it.

"Good morning," Ted's voice called out cheerily. "Headache gone?"

Her fingers tightened on the receiver. "All gone. I'm feeling much better. How'd your night go?"

"Biz–zee, in and out of bed all night, but nothing too serious. Mostly minor stuff. I'm hoping to catch a couple of catnaps today. Think you could get an extended lunch hour? I thought maybe I could con you into picking up a couple of burger baskets and bringing them over to the station."

She glanced at her desk calendar. "Sure, I guess I could do that."

"Good. I talk about you all the time, but none of these guys I work with thinks you're real. I want them to meet you."

"You're kidding, right?"

"No, that's the truth. See you about twelve?"

"Ah, sure. Twelve will be fine, Ted. I'll be there."

ᵃ

"I'm here to see Ted Benay," Sammy told the fireman who opened the door when she rang the outside buzzer at noon.

With a congenial smile he eyed her then motioned her inside, closing the door behind her. "So you're Sammy?"

She nodded awkwardly. "Yes, is he here?"

"Sammy!" Ted rushed into the waiting room and latched onto her hand. "You made it."

Three other firemen hurried in and gave her the once-over as the first one had done. "Well, I'll be," one of them said, nudging Ted's arm. "She *is* real. You've got yourself a girlfriend."

"A good-lookin' girlfriend," the third one added.

"Too good-lookin' for the likes of this ugly guy," the fourth one added, ramming his fist into Ted's arm. "Must be all that great fireman's pay you're hoardin' in your attic that attracted her."

"Actually it's my animal magnetism that attracted her."

Slipping his arm around her waist and drawing her to him protectively, Ted rolled his eyes. "Don't listen to this bunch of old windbags, Sammy. They've been here way too long, heard too many fire bells, and it's affected their thinking."

Grinning, Captain Grey joined them. "I have to admit, Ted, I never expected such a beautiful young lady to take up with the likes of you."

Unable to think of a thing to say and overwhelmed with all their undeserved flattery, she simply smiled at each one before turning her smile on Ted.

He drew her closer. "See what I have to put up with, Sammy? Can you imagine having to spend twenty-four-hour shifts with this bunch of characters?"

"Come on, fellas." The captain motioned them toward the day room. "Might be a good idea if we gave them some privacy. Looks like Sammy's brought their lunch."

"Nice to have met you," she called out as the smiling group trooped out of the room.

"Sorry. I hope they didn't embarrass you. I'm kinda their pet-pick-on project. They meant no harm." Ted gestured toward a small desk along the wall. "Why don't we sit over there?"

She handed the carryout sack to him then scooted into a chair. "I wasn't embarrassed, and I hope you weren't either. I could tell they really like you."

He ripped the bag open, distributed their burger baskets, then pulled up a chair beside her. "They're a great bunch of guys. I'm used to their ribbing. Mmm, this smells good."

"I know you like grilled onions. I had them add a few extras."

He gave her wink. "You're my kind of woman. Thanks." Without asking, he bowed his head and simply said, "Thank You, God, for this food and Sammy's willingness to bring it."

How good it felt to know that, despite the way Ted felt about his sister's heart, he was still on praying ground.

"I was hoping you'd come," he said finally, breaking the silence that seemed to wedge itself between them. "I owe you an apology. For ranting the way I did yesterday. I had no right to lay my feelings on you like that. You were a real sport about it."

You still can't see how unreasonable you are? Your sister wanted to donate her heart. It was such an unselfish thing to do. Because of her and others like her, there are people like me who are able to live and breathe and enjoy life for a few more years than we may not have had otherwise. You should have respected her for it.

"My mom and I can't even be in the same room without getting into a disagreement over—well, you know what."

Sammy picked a dill pickle slice off her burger and placed it on her plate. "Don't you think that's a bit sad? You said it's been over three years since you lost your sister. You can't unring a bell, Ted. What's done is done."

"That may be true, but I want to make sure they don't volunteer my organs when *I'm* gone. I want my body to remain intact. I still get the willies when I visit Tiger's grave, just thinking about it. But no more of this unpleasant talk, okay? Subject finished. As you said, you can't unring a bell. Tomorrow's my day off. Got any plans for supper?"

"Not plans exactly, but I was going to stop by the store and pick up a small ham. The children love ham and beans. I usually put them on to cook before I leave for work and let them simmer all day."

"Ham and beans? I love ham and beans!"

"Does that mean you're trying to wheedle an invitation?"

"Would it work if I said yes?"

His silly expression made her laugh. "Only if you stay to help with the cleanup."

He stuck out his hand. "Deal."

"That means you'll have to put up with the three munchkins again, and you'd better come prepared to play catch with Simon."

"I'll be there. Six?"

"Six."

❧

All the next day Sammy watched the clock, wondering if she'd added enough water to the beans, turned the oven up too high, sprinkled on too much seasoning. But when she rushed into her apartment at five thirty, lifted the lid, and tasted a spoonful of the perfectly cooked and seasoned ham and beans, she knew she had done everything right. The ham was tender enough to fall apart, the beans were just the right texture, and the aroma was inviting.

With Ted's old ball glove already on his hand, Simon parted the curtains and peered out the window. "How come he's not here yet?"

Sammy gave the boy a hug. "Because it's not six."

"He can't play ball with you, Simon," Tina told him from her place on the sofa. "He's gonna read a book to me and Harley."

"No, he's not! He said he—"

"Whoa, you two. If Ted heard you arguing like that, I doubt he'd play catch *or* read a book." Sammy lifted Harley, straddling the child's legs over one hip. "I'm glad you kids like Ted, but when he gets here let's give him some space, okay?" When the children gave her a reluctant nod, she quickly placed Harley on the sofa beside Tina and hurried into the kitchen to prepare the cornbread, mince the raw onion, and set the table.

"Mmm, mmm. Ham and beans. Does that ever smell good."

Surprised to hear Ted's voice behind her, Sammy swung around quickly. "I didn't know you were here yet."

"Simon was standing in the doorway when I arrived. He let me in." He glanced around the kitchen. "What can I do to help?"

"Not a thing. Everything's ready."

The five of them laughed their way through dinner as Ted told story after story of things that happened to him when he was growing up. Sammy was filled with both joy and regret as she listened and watched the happy expression on the children's faces. Joy because they were having so much fun with Ted and regret when she realized how much they'd missed by not having a father figure in their lives.

"Tell you what, Simon," Ted told the boy once their last bite of dessert had been consumed. "Give me fifteen minutes to help your aunt clean up the kitchen, and we'll go out onto the parking lot and play some catch."

"But Harley and me wanted you to read us a book."

With a consoling smile, Ted turned to Tina. "I'll read to you as soon as Simon and I finish playing catch, okay?"

Sammy was relieved when Tina didn't fuss and simply nodded. She was sure Ted had his fill of bickering when he was home. He didn't need anymore.

❧

"Are you gonna move in and live with us?" Simon asked Ted as the two walked out to the parking lot.

Taken aback by the boy's question, Ted stared at him. "Move in with you and your aunt? Why would you think something like that?"

The boy gave a nonchalant shrug. "All my mom's boyfriends moved in with us."

Ted ached for Simon. What a sad, confused life that boy must have had before he and his sisters came to live with Sammy. "No, I'm not going to move in with you. I'm not going to live with any woman unless we're married."

"Are you gonna marry Aunt Sammy?"

Ted's jaw dropped. He'd been put on the spot by a nine-year-old, and he had no idea how to answer.

"If you married Aunt Sammy, *then* you could live with us."

Deciding to sidestep the question, Ted reached out and tousled the boy's hair. "Did we come out here to talk or play ball? It'll be dark soon."

Simon smiled up at him. "Play ball."

Ted backed away, pulled a brand-new, shiny white ball from his jacket pocket and gently tossed it to Simon. "Okay, let's play ball."

❧

Sammy braced her arms on the window sill and gazed dreamily at the game of catch going on in the parking lot. She tried to imagine what it would be like if she were married to Ted and stood watching him play ball with their own son. *Come on, girl. Get back to reality,* she told herself, shaking her head to dismiss the thoughts. *Dream all you want, but don't expect your dreams to come true. There are far too many obstacles in your way.*

Ted burst through the door with Simon at his heels. "Whew! Simon and I worked up a sweat. Got any of that iced tea left?"

Sammy hurried toward the kitchen. "Coming right up."

Ted took the glass from her hand then sat down on the sofa, squeezing himself between two giggling little girls. "Okay, which book are we going to read?"

Still giggling, Tina pointed to a book on the coffee table.

He reached for it and gazed at the cover. "*The Little Engine That Could*? Sounds like a good book to me. Is this your favorite?"

Both girls nodded.

"As soon as Ted finishes the book, it's off to bed for all three of you." As eager to hear him read the story as the girls were, Sammy sat down in the wooden rocking chair she'd rescued from the dumpster and waited.

❧

Ted glanced her way as he opened the book. She was so beautiful, so sweet. Suddenly Simon's question popped into his head. Though he had to admit he felt a real attraction to Sammy, he hadn't thought seriously of marrying her. But now, sitting there with her across from him, smiling at him with that smile that drove him crazy, the idea of being married to her had great appeal. Just then Harley crawled onto his lap and leaned her head against his chest, and he remembered that marrying Sammy could mean a package deal. The idea of spending the rest of his life with Sammy—and possibly three children that weren't his—lost some of its luster.

"I'm not in any rush to get away," he said when he finished

reading. "Is there anything I can do to help you get them ready for bed?" He closed the book and put it back on the table.

"Not really. They're all old enough to get into their jammies by themselves. I just need to make sure they brush their teeth and—" She paused. "It won't take long. I—I have something important to tell you. Why don't you relax and wait for me?"

"Good idea." Glad for the opportunity to spend more time with her, Ted told the children good night then leaned back against the sofa, closing his eyes.

Sammy appeared again fifteen minutes later. "All tucked in. Thanks for being so patient." She sat down beside him and smiled. "For someone who never wanted kids, you're pretty good with children. Those three adore you."

He shrugged. "Funny thing is, I enjoy being around them. Especially Simon. Tiger loved children. She always wanted a big family, a whole houseful of kids." Ted slipped his arm about her shoulders. "Since you're the children's caretaker and your sister might never come back after them, if the right man came along, would you consider marrying him?"

She let out a sharp breath. "Do you honestly think any man would want to take on a wife and three children who weren't even hers?"

"I was asking you a hypothetical question."

"Hypothetical, huh? Okay, then my hypothetical answer would be yes—*if* the right man came along and *if* he loved me and shared my faith and *if* he was willing to help me provide a good, loving, stable home for them. But I doubt that's going to happen. Not many men would be crazy enough to take on that kind of responsibility."

"Yeah, you may be right." He wanted so much to be able to tell her how attracted he was to her, but getting seriously involved with Sammy would mean a bigger commitment than he might be prepared to give. Yet he couldn't walk away from her. *Face it, buddy. You're not only attracted to Sammy, but you're in love with her! You're even thinking the M word.*

"Oh," he said, snapping his fingers and hoping to change the subject, "you said you had something to tell me. What is it?"

Sammy sucked in a deep breath. *No need to tell you about my transplant now. It looks as if our relationship is doomed since you just agreed with me that any man would be crazy to take on my unconventional little family.* "Never mind. It wasn't important."

He eyed her suspiciously. "You sure? You made it sound important."

"Trust me. It's nothing you need to know."

His shoulders rose in a nonchalant shrug. "Okay."

Sammy winced as his arm tightened around her. *Now what do I do? Try to end things as quickly as possible to avoid the agony of putting off the inevitable? Or simply let things take their course and enjoy the ride until it blows up in my face? Either way I'm going to be miserable when this sweet relationship with Ted comes to an end.*

He cupped his free hand over hers, his thumb gently massaging her knuckles. "I'm pulling an extra shift again tomorrow. That means I can't see you for two whole days. I may have withdrawal pains."

Sammy gazed at their joined hands, enjoying his touch. If only it could be that way forever. "Someone sick?"

"Naw, one of the guys needs time off to go to his folks' fiftieth wedding anniversary celebration. Fifty years with the same person—wow! Think you could spend fifty years with the same guy?"

"If I were married to the man of God's choosing."

"I'm in awe of your faith, Sammy. You seem to trust God for everything. Don't you ever get mad? Throw things? Pout?"

She pulled her hand away and fiddled with the neck of her shirt, checking to make sure the top button had remained firmly lodged in its buttonhole. "I'd be lying if I said I didn't." She managed a slight snicker. "Well, I don't throw things, but I do get pretty upset sometimes, and I have been known to pout when things haven't gone my way. But God is faithful. He always sees me through." *I'm counting on Him to see me through whatever happens with you.*

"He's seen me though all my troubles, too, except for one. I don't know where He was when that one happened. He sure wasn't listening to me."

"Your sister?"

"Yeah, God really let me down on that one."

"Maybe *you* let *Him* down."

"Me? How?"

"By making such a big issue out of something that seemed important enough to your sister that she signed a donor card." The frown and look of almost despair he gave her made her wonder if she'd overstepped some invisible line.

"Look, Sammy—I know you mean well. But you've never had a loved one's heart taken from them as I have, or, believe me, you'd feel differently about things. I did the research. I've seen the pictures. I know what that type of surgery looks like. Until you've walked in those shoes—"

"I *have* walked in those shoes!" she blurted out.

Ted spun around to face her. "What do you mean, you've walked in those shoes?"

Her heart racing and her fingers trembling, with tears she unfastened the top button on her shirt, spreading the tips of the collar far apart. "See! See this scar? You should recognize it, Ted. You said you did the research!"

All color drained from his face as he stared at the scar. "You've had a—a heart transplant?"

Lifting her chin to allow him a better view, she wept openly, nearly shouting her words. "Yes, I've had a heart transplant! Thanks to people like your sister, who unselfishly donate their organs, I was able to receive a donor heart, and it saved my life. I waited over two years for this heart, Ted. Two long, scary years. So, yes, I *do* know what it's like to have your heart taken from you. But, praise God, mine was replaced with a healthy one someone was no longer able to use!"

Visibly shaken by her revelation, Ted stood and began to pace about the room, raking his fingers through his hair. "Why didn't you tell me? I had no idea—"

"Tell you? After the way you've carried on about your sister's heart?"

His face drawn and contorted, he stopped pacing and spread his arms open wide. "So now what am I supposed to do? For all I know, that could be my sister's heart beating in your chest."

Brushing away tears with the back of her hand, she shook her head firmly. "That's not likely, Ted. I was living in Denver at the time."

"That's a relief." He grabbed up his ball glove and headed for the door. "This is maddening. I've got to get out of here."

She hurried after him. "I'm sorry this is upsetting you, but I'm glad you know. I've hated keeping it a secret."

"That was no secret you were keeping, Sammy. It was a bombshell!" With that, he yanked open the door and disappeared. A few seconds later, she heard the tires on his truck squeal as he left the parking lot.

Ted was gone.

Probably for good.

seven

Two weeks passed, and still no word came from Ted. Though Sammy wore a pleasant smile around the children, she ached inside. There was no excuse for what she had done. She knew how strongly Ted felt. She should have told him the day she'd learned about his sister's death and faced up to his reaction, no matter how upsetting it might be. Instead of waiting and blurting it out as she had, with no warning or forethought leading up to it to soften its impact.

But that was hindsight, and she had to admit the few weeks she'd had with Ted were the best weeks of her life. She thought they'd been good for him, too, but apparently not good enough for him to put aside his feelings of resentment and anger.

"When is Ted gonna come and play catch with me?" Simon asked late one evening as Sammy knelt beside his bed. "He said he'd come back, but he hasn't."

Swallowing at the lump in her throat that seemed to have become a permanent fixture, Sammy bent and kissed the boy's forehead. "I don't know when Ted is coming back, Simon. I miss him, too."

Turning away from her, he flipped over onto his side, tugging the quilt with him. "People never come back when they say they will. That's what my mom said, too, and she never came back."

"I wish I had an answer for you, honey, but I don't. But I love you, Simon, and I promise you the only reason I'd ever leave you is if your mother comes back. But even if she doesn't, I'm going to be right here beside you. You do believe me, don't you?"

"I guess so," he barely whispered.

"God will never leave you either. No matter what. Simon, do you hear me?" She nudged his shoulder lightly, only to find he'd fallen asleep. She wasn't even sure he'd heard what she said.

≈

"Phone call," Tiffany told her the next afternoon as Sammy passed by the reception desk. "They asked for Rosalinda Samuel. I'd nearly forgotten your real name since everyone calls you Sammy. You can take it here if you want."

"Thanks, but I'll take it in my office."

"You not feeling well, Sammy? I've never seen you so down in the dumps before. You and that boyfriend of yours break up?"

Sammy pasted on a fake smile. "Just been busy, that's all." She hurried past Tiffany's desk, made her way through the maze of cubicles that lined the walls and stepped into her office. "This is Rosalinda Samuel. How may I help you?"

"Miss Samuel. This is Dr. Bettenburg's office in Denver. We keep hearing from the doctor's office of the person who donated their heart to you. It seems your donor's mother wants desperately to meet you and see how you're doing. Her doctor had explained the anonymity clause to her, but the woman refuses to take no for an answer. Dr. Bettenburg and her doctor have finally agreed that our office should phone you to see if you have any interest in meeting with this person."

Sammy tapped her pencil idly on the desk. "I wouldn't mind meeting with her—in fact, I'd like to thank her—but as you know, I no longer live in Denver."

"Oh, she doesn't live in Denver either. She lives in Tennessee. Smith Springs, Tennessee. Is that anywhere near Nashville?"

"I think so. I'm not sure."

"Do you want us to call her and give her your number, or would you prefer to call Barbara McCoy directly?"

Pulling a fresh sheet off the notepad, Sammy poised her pencil. "Give me the number. I'll call her." She wrote down the number then added the name Barbara McCoy.

"By the way, Miss Samuel, how are you and that heart of yours getting along? We miss seeing you here in our Denver office."

"It's doing just fine. I can't tell you how grateful I am to the donor and to Dr. Bettenburg. I can hardly wait to talk to Mrs. McCoy. Thank you for calling. Give my best to the doctor."

Before she could dial the number, her phone rang again. This time it was her mother.

"Hi, sweetie. Any word from Ted?"

"No, nothing, not that I expected to hear from him."

"I know I warned you not to tell him, but I was wrong. Perhaps it would have been better if you'd told him earlier."

"I know, Mom, but that's hindsight."

"Telling him at the very beginning could have saved you both a lot of grief."

"But if I'd told him, then we wouldn't have become acquainted, and I wouldn't have had all those wonderful times with him. I wouldn't give those up for anything. Those times will stay with me forever."

"I'm glad you had those times, too, but I worry about you, dear. You *are* taking your medication, aren't you? You know how important that is."

"Yes, Mom, I'm taking my medication. You worry too much. I do have something to tell you though." She explained the call she'd received from Dr. Bettenburg's office.

"You're going to call her? That Mrs. McCoy?"

"Yes, I was about to dial her number when your call came in."

"Let me know what happens, okay?"

"You'll be the first to know."

"I love you, Sammy. Give the kids a kiss and a hug for me."

"I will. Love you, too, Mom. 'Bye."

Sammy broke the connection and sat staring at the phone for several minutes. Finally she dialed the number then sat back and waited while it rang. One ring. Two. Three. Then, gasping for breath, a woman's voice answered. "McCoy residence."

"Mrs. McCoy, this is Rosalinda Samuel. The nurse in Dr. Bettenburg's Denver office called and said you were trying to reach me." Was that weeping she heard on the other end of the line?

"I can't thank you enough for calling. We lost our precious daughter a little over three years ago. She'd signed a donor card. We've always wanted to find the person who received her heart, but there are rules of anonymity about those things. I can't tell you how happy I am to finally be talking to you."

Sammy clutched the phone tightly, her own eyes filled with tears. "I'm glad to be talking to you, too, Mrs. McCoy. I've wanted to thank you. I can only imagine how hard all of this has been on you. Losing a child has to be one of the worst ordeals a person would have to endure. The nurse who phoned me said you lived at Smith Springs?"

"Yes, we live on the lake. It's such a beautiful spot. I'm sure you're busy, but I was wondering if you might be able to come down and spend a little time with my husband and me? Maybe Sunday afternoon. We're about twenty miles southeast of you. The Murfreesboro Pike will bring you right to us. I'd offer to come up to Nashville, but I recently had a knee replacement and am not getting around too well."

"I think I could work that out. What time should I be there?"

"Anytime will be fine."

Sammy glanced at her watch. If she left right after church on Sunday, she could be there by no later than one o'clock, maybe even earlier, depending on the traffic. "I'll try to be there around one, but you'd better give me directions."

The woman gave her specific instructions, even telling her the color of the paint on the houses at the intersections, then added, "You have no idea how grateful I am to God for bringing us together. If it weren't for His love and mercies, my husband and I couldn't have made it through our tragedy."

Sammy felt an instant kinship with Mrs. McCoy. "That's the way I feel, too. My faith in God is the most important thing in my life."

"I think you and I are going to be the best of friends, Rosalinda. We'll see you on Sunday."

"Yes, Sunday." An overwhelming joy filled Sammy's heart as she hung up the phone. At last she was going to meet her donor's family.

His brother was sitting on the couch wearing a stained T-shirt and a pair of tattered jeans, looking bored and staring at the TV when Ted strolled into the living room at the end of his shift. "Hey, bro, what's happening? Had your breakfast yet?" When Albert slowly turned in his direction, he caught sight of an overgrowth of beard that appeared to be about three days' worth. "What's the matter? Your razor on the fritz?"

"Nope, it's working fine."

Ted sat down beside him. "So what's with the beard?"

"Just figured it was a good time to grow one."

"What's the matter, Albert? You still having trouble finding a job? I know you've been out on a bunch of job interviews."

Albert glanced toward the kitchen then leaned toward Ted. "Nobody wants me. I'm either too old or too qualified. I may end up flipping burgers. But please don't say anything to Wilma about it. She's upset enough with me already."

"What's happened to you, Albert? You used to be top salesman every month, won a car for your outstanding sales record, then took over the management of that car dealership in Miami."

His brother shrugged. "Lost my zip, I guess. I can't seem to do anything right anymore. My wife thinks I'm a loser. My kids are out of control. My bank account is depleted. My credit card maxed out. I just don't care."

He reached for the can of beer he'd left on the coffee table, but Ted stopped him. "How long has that been going on? The drinking?"

Albert's brows rose. "I may drink, but I don't have a drinking problem."

"Hey, buddy, this is me you're talking to. Ted, your brother. I'm not here to condemn you. I'm here to help you." He gently placed his hand on Albert's wrist. "Is this the real reason you lost your job?"

After a few moments of silence, Albert lifted his face to Ted's, his eyes filled with tears. "Yeah, I kinda let my drinking take over my life. I'm not sure you ever noticed because you were so grief stricken, but our precious sister's death was hard on me, too. I think I took it harder than anyone realized. Me included."

"And I shut you out, didn't I?" Ted slipped his arm around his brother's shoulders. "I wish you'd confided in me sooner. You need help, man. I'm here for you now."

Albert rubbed at his eyes with his sleeve. "I couldn't ask you for help. You're already letting my family live here with you and paying for most of the groceries. That's far more than I deserve."

A lump rose in Ted's throat, and he felt like a heel for criticizing his brother and his family. "What I'm doing for you doesn't amount to a drop in the bucket. Together we'll see this thing through. Whatever I have, whatever you need, is yours."

Weeping like a baby, Albert buried his head in his hands. "Thanks, Ted."

"As I said, man, I'm here for you." He paused. "I assume you and your family haven't been attending church, right?"

Albert nodded. "We dropped out sometime ago. I haven't prayed in years. I figured God didn't want to hear from me. Somehow it seemed arrogant to get drunk all week then go to church on Sunday and pretend everything was right between me and the Lord."

Ted gestured toward his brother's dowdy apparel. "From the looks of things, I'd say you don't have any plans for today. How about going to see Pastor Day with me? I've heard they have a great twelve-step program at his church. Not just for those who have trouble with drinking but also for anyone whose life is out of whack. And don't worry about a place to live. You can stay with me as long as you like. And as to finances? I've got a little money saved up. You can have what you need now and pay me back when you get a job."

"You'd—you'd do that for me?"

"Sure I would. You're my brother. We brothers have to stick together." Ted took the half-empty beer can from the table and carried it to the bathroom, emptying it in the sink, then brought it back and placed it in the metal wastebasket by the desk. "Go get you a cup of coffee while I phone the pastor."

❧

In some ways it seemed the week would never end; in other ways it almost flew by. But still no word from Ted. Three times Sammy drove by the fire station, and three times she saw his truck parked in the lot, but she never stopped. It was obvious she was out of Ted's life for good. To make matters worse, the children kept asking for him.

"Maybe you should call him," her mother said as the two stood in the church's welcome center on Sunday morning. "Men are the world's worst when it comes to admitting they've made a mistake. Perhaps Ted is missing you as much as you miss him, but he's having trouble admitting it."

Sammy shook her head. "No, Mom. You don't know him the way I do. He was adamant about his opinion on his sister's heart being taken from her and given away. You should have heard him talk about it. He even researched the procedure."

"Somehow that doesn't sound like the Ted you've told me about. You described Ted as being compassionate, kind, gentle. I can't imagine his getting so upset he'd walk out on you."

"I'm convinced it was because he knew each time he looked at me, he'd be reminded of his sister and what had happened to her."

Her mother shrugged. "The whole thing is so sad. I just hope he comes to his senses. I hate seeing you like this."

"Could we not talk about it anymore, please? Are you sure you don't mind keeping the children this afternoon?"

"Of course I don't mind. We'll have fun. Don't you worry about a thing. Just concentrate on having a good time with Mr. and Mrs. McCoy."

Since the church service ended a little earlier than usual, Sammy decided to stop long enough to pick up a sandwich and fill her car's tank at the convenience store before driving on to Smith Springs. But as she headed for the door to pay for her gas, someone called out her name.

eight

It was Captain Grey. "Well, hello, Sammy. How've you been?"

Though Sammy was glad to see him, she knew their pleasantries would eventually turn to Ted. "I'm doing okay. How about you?"

"Me? Other than covering an extra shift today, I'm doin' just fine." He took hold of her arm, pulling her to one side to let a customer pass, then asked quietly, "It's none of my business, but did you and Ted break up? He's been like a bearcat for the past couple of weeks. Barks at everyone. Stays to himself. Grumbles about everything. That's not Ted's style. All the guys are worried about him. I even asked him about it, but all he did was shrug."

"I guess you could say we broke up. He pretty much walked out on me."

"*He* walked out on *you*? That's strange. He'd told some of the guys he was thinking about asking you to marry him."

Sammy's jaw dropped. "He did?"

"You didn't know? He never said anything about it to you?"

"No. I was half hoping we were heading in that direction, but—" She paused, wondering if she'd said too much already.

"I know it's none of my business, but I'd like to see the two of you get back together. I'll keep you both in my prayers."

"Thanks. I'd appreciate it."

He held up a carton of milk then gestured toward a red

truck parked in front of the store, bearing the Nashville Fire Department emblem on its door. "I'd better get this to our cook, or we won't have any lunch. He needs it for the gravy. Want me to tell Ted hello for you?"

She shook her head. "No, I doubt he would care, but it was nice to see you. Have a good day."

He nodded. "You, too."

She watched until his truck disappeared around the corner. He said Ted was thinking of asking her to marry him? She was that close to winning the heart of the man she'd hoped to marry and lost him? *Lord, why? Why couldn't Ted see the good his sister's act had done? Why couldn't he be proud of her instead of being upset with her and her decision? And with me? And why can't he stop questioning You?*

Blinking back tears, Sammy selected her sandwich from the refrigerated case, added a soft drink, and paid for her purchases. *Forget about Ted. Think of something pleasant,* she told herself, squaring her shoulders as she headed toward her car. *Smile. Be thankful. You're going to meet some wonderful people today—people who are proud of the fact that their child was willing to donate her organs to someone who needed them.*

By following the directions Mrs. McCoy had given her, Sammy found their place with no difficulty, even though it was located in a densely wooded area on a road high up on a hill overlooking the lake. The McCoys were standing on the deck, smiling, waiting for her when she arrived.

Barbara McCoy, a slight woman with graying hair who looked to be in her midfifties, threw her arms around Sammy and gave her a hug. "I can't believe you're actually here!" Then, turning to her husband, she added, "Isn't she beautiful, Carl?"

"She sure is." Extending his hand, he greeted Sammy with a warm smile. "Nice to meet you, Rosalinda."

Bracing herself with her cane, Barbara McCoy took hold of Sammy's arm and limped toward the door. "Come on inside. Let me get you a nice glass of iced tea."

Once the three were seated comfortably in the living room, Barbara gestured toward a photograph prominently displayed on the mantel. "I remember the day my precious daughter told me she had signed a donor card. Tanny was so afraid I'd be mad at her for doing it without asking me."

"Tanny? How beautiful. That was your daughter's name?"

"Yes, Tanny. She always liked it." The woman paused, as if to gather her emotions before going on. "I—I told her I wasn't mad at her. I was proud of her for doing it. I told her Carl and I had signed one, too."

Carl took his wife's hand, gently cradling it in his own. "Barbara and I figured we'd be the ones to go first, but I guess God had other plans."

Barbara's face brightened somewhat. "Tell us all about yourself, Rosalinda. We want to hear everything."

For the next few minutes, Sammy told them about the trouble she'd had as a child with rheumatic fever and how it had affected her heart and weakened it. "I was on a waiting list for two years before I got the call to"—she stopped mid-sentence, aware of the impact her next few words would have on Tanny's parents—"to report to the hospital."

"That was the night our daughter lost her life." Barbara pulled a tissue from her pocket and dabbed at her eyes. A gentle smile tilted the corners of her lips. "I know this sounds silly, but may I feel your heart beating? Tanny's heart?"

So touched by the woman's request she could barely speak, Sammy nodded, took her hand, placed it next to her heart, and held it there. Her heart seemed to thunder in response, as if just by being Tanny's heart it could sense Barbara's presence.

Barbara's eyes widened. "I can feel it! I'm actually feeling my daughter's heart beating. Oh, this is a true miracle!"

Sammy struggled to contain the pent-up tears, but they spilled down her cheeks. "Yes, it is a miracle. If your daughter hadn't signed that card—"

"But she did, Rosalinda, and I was so proud of her for doing it. In many ways you remind me of her. I'm thankful her heart went to you. I have a feeling you're as kind and unselfish as she was." Slowly Barbara pulled away her hand. "Thank you for letting me feel the beating of her heart. It's a moment I'll treasure forever. We must stay in touch. I can't tell you how good it is to have you here with us." She turned to her husband. "Isn't it, Carl?"

He nodded then smiled at Sammy. "My wife has been hoping and praying for this day ever since Tanny left us. There's no way we can tell you how thankful we are that you agreed to meet with us."

"And come all the way to Smith Springs to do it," Barbara added. "Carl is driving me up to Nashville in a couple of weeks to see my doctor. Maybe the three of us could have lunch together."

"I'd love it. You have my phone number. Just give me a call." Sammy liked these two. They were such a nice couple. What a warm, loving home they must have provided for their daughter.

"Carl, why don't you take Sammy's picture with that new

digital camera I gave you for your birthday?"

"Great idea." Carl hurried to the bookcase. "Maybe I can get a picture of the two of you together."

Sammy held up her hand, a grin etched on her face. "You can only take my picture if you e-mail me copies."

Carl nodded. "You got it. Now smile for me."

Once the flash had gone off, he motioned Sammy to scoot closer to Barbara. "Oh, that'll make a nice picture."

Again Sammy's heart seemed to thunder in her chest.

After Carl had taken several more pictures, he put the camera back in its place. "You ladies sure looked good together."

From somewhere in the direction of the kitchen, a door slammed. "Hey, anybody home?"

nine

The smile on Barbara's face widened.

"We're in the living room, son," Carl called out, glancing at his wife.

Sammy sucked in a breath and then held it. *That voice! It couldn't be!*

"I know it's been awhile, and I should have—" Their visitor stopped midsentence, his startled gaze going to Sammy then to Barbara, to Carl, and back to Sammy as he entered the room.

Barbara reached out her hands. "I had no idea you were coming today. Come here. I want you to meet someone."

No, no, it can't be! Sammy, feeling as if her breath had been knocked out of her, managed a faint smile as the pieces of an unknown puzzle suddenly fit together. "Ted?"

Barbara turned to face her. "You two know each other?"

"Sammy?" Ted rushed across the room. "I don't get it. What are you doing here? How do you know my parents?"

"Sammy? I thought her name was Rosalinda."

"It is," Sammy confessed with a nod toward Carl, her gaze still fixed on Ted. "Rosalinda is my given name, but almost everyone calls me Sammy."

Carl leaned forward in his chair, his attention going back to his son. "You mean she didn't tell you?"

"Tell me what?"

Barbara latched onto Sammy's hand, holding it tight. "That

she's the one who received your sister's heart."

The color drained from Ted's face. "What? No. That can't be. What are you talking about?"

"I'm as surprised as you are!" Sammy thought for a moment before speaking. "It's true, Ted. I *am* the recipient of your sister's heart. But, until I saw you walk through that door and I put two and two together, I had no idea the heart that was keeping me alive belonged to your sister."

Ted dropped down in a chair, his long arms dangling at his sides, his voice tinged with anger. "This is too much."

Barbara's arm circled Sammy's shoulders protectively. "Don't you dare be upset with this sweet girl. I believe her when she says she didn't know whose heart she had. I'm the one who contacted her when I finally convinced the doctor who operated on your sister to get in touch with the recipient. He told her we'd like to meet her, and asked her to contact us. Sammy, being the kind, gentle, understanding person she is, called me. We talked, and she agreed to meet with us. If I'd thought you would have behaved yourself and not gone into a tirade, I'd have invited you to be here when she came, but you'd made your feelings perfectly clear. I had no idea how you'd treat her."

Carl motioned toward Ted. "But you still haven't told us how the two of you know each other. I'm sure your mother is as curious as I am."

"We've been dating."

Barbara's eyes widened. "You have? You and Rosalinda?"

"Yeah, we met on a riverboat ride." Ted sent Sammy a sheepish nod. "I thought she was about the prettiest and nicest girl I'd ever met."

"I wish I'd told you in the beginning, Ted." Sammy fingered

her collar. "Then maybe we would never have—" She took a breath. "But having a secondhand heart isn't something you casually bring up in conversation. A lot of emotional baggage comes along with knowing you're alive only because someone else died—not to mention the terrible scar it leaves, the medication, the frequent trips to the doctor for checkups, the limited life span. As you once told me, some people consider the whole procedure unacceptable—you being one of them. But I honestly had no idea of all this." She nodded toward his parents.

"I hope you didn't behave as badly about it in front of Rosalinda as you did with us," Barbara said, her voice wavering with emotion. "Your words hurt me, Ted. They hurt your dad, too. We only did what your sister wanted."

"You could have intervened."

"And go against Tanny's wishes? No! When she signed that donor card, she made it clear that's what she wanted. As her mother, I felt compelled to let her have her way."

For a moment Ted stared at his mother without speaking. When he rose, his gaze traveled to Sammy. "I'm glad you were able to have a heart transplant, Sammy, but it should never have been my sister's." He turned and rushed out the front door.

Sammy started to go after him, but Barbara grabbed her hand. "No, leave him alone. You'll only get hurt."

"If I'd had any idea you were Ted's parents, I wouldn't have come without telling him. But I didn't know. Honest, I didn't." Sammy shook her head. "I'm so confused. Ted's name is Benay. Yours is McCoy. You live in Smith Springs. He lives in Nashville. Your daughter died in Nashville, but I received her heart in Denver."

Carl gave her a kindly smile. "I'm Ted's stepfather. His real father was killed in an industrial accident when Tanny and Ted were barely two. Barbara and I were married a couple of years later. Though I'm the only father the children have ever known, we decided they should keep the Benay name in honor of their father. We lived in Nashville until the company I worked for went bankrupt a few years ago and I got a job here in Smith Springs."

"Didn't Ted ever mention his sister?"

Sammy rubbed at her eyes. "Yes, Barbara, he did, but he always called her Tiger, not Tanny."

"That was his pet name for her from the time they were little, when he first began to talk."

"If only I'd known. I'm sure Ted loves the Lord, but he's having a hard time getting past God taking his sister."

Barbara sighed. "I know. Losing his twin has been agony for him. I think the real problem is the guilt he feels because he was driving the car. He's always felt responsible for her death. I'm not so sure it's God he's upset with. I think he's mad at himself and can't understand why God would have let that accident happen."

Carl nodded in agreement. "That boy has really struggled with his part in his sister's death. You know what they say. There's a special bond between twins. I think the day Tanny died, a bit of Ted died, too. He's never stopped blaming himself."

Sammy considered both Carl's and Barbara's words. "So many things have confused me about Ted, but what you've told me of his terrible inner struggle over the accident helps me understand him better."

"We pray constantly for him, that he'll wake up and see

how unreasonable he's been and how many people he's hurt by shutting them out. It wasn't Ted's fault the accident happened. It was the driver of the other car's fault." Barbara gestured toward the picture on the mantel. "Our lovely daughter's life was snuffed out that day, but in some ways she's still with us because of you and your need for a heart. How many people can say that of a loved one they've lost? If Ted could only see that, he'd be proud to know the woman he's become fond of is alive and well because of his sister."

"But I still don't understand how I ended up being the recipient of your daughter's heart when she died in Tennessee and I lived in Denver. Since Denver is such a large city, I always assumed my heart came from there."

Barbara clasped Sammy's hand in hers. "That part confused me, too, so I asked the surgeon's office about it. They said it's best to get a donor's heart to the recipient as quickly as possible. So donor hearts are flown all over the world and don't always stay in the area where the donor lives."

"That's why I ended up receiving a donor heart from Tennessee even though I lived in Denver? Amazing."

"Yes, it is amazing. I look at it as another one of God's miracles." She sighed. "We have to continue to pray for Ted."

In awe of what had just happened, Sammy turned to stare at the front door. "Yes, we have to."

❧

Ted drove like a madman, his foot pressing harder on the gas pedal than it should as he made his way back to Nashville. Why did it have to be Sammy who had his sister's heart? How could he bear to see her again? And why hadn't she told him earlier about her heart? He could understand her reluctance to tell him when they first met, but how about later when they got to be friends? Would it have been so hard to have told him? He was a reasonable sort of guy. Easygoing. Not normally upset by unexpected things. Most of the time anyway. But the thought of her having someone else's heart beating in her chest, and now finding out it was his sister's— it was more than he could take. He would never forget the accident he'd tried so hard to erase from his memory.

When he reached Nashville, he pulled into the gym out on Nolensville Pike to work off some steam, *Funny*, he thought as he pulled on his shorts and headed for the exercise equipment, *when I got out of bed this morning, my goal was to go visit my folks and make peace with them. That's a far cry from what happened. They're probably more upset with me now than they were before I got there.*

He yanked a towel from the shelf and tossed it over his shoulder. *And I had hoped she was the right woman for me. Now I don't know what to do. Every time I look at her, all I'll be able to think about is Tiger's heart.* Lifting his eyes heavenward, he whispered, "Why, God? Why did You have to let this happen? You could have performed miracles—let Tiger live *and* healed Sammy. What was Your purpose in all of this? I just don't get it."

"Don't get what?"

Ted spun around, embarrassed that someone had overheard him. "Oh, hi, Jake. I didn't know you worked out here."

"I do, but not as often as I'd like. For some reason, my girlfriend can't understand why a guy my age would enjoy lifting weights and running on a treadmill." Jake gave Ted a playful jab to his shoulder. "You and Sammy make up yet?"

Ted frowned. "No, I'm afraid not."

Jake looked at him. "Take it from me—if you like that little gal, tell her you're sorry for whatever happened between you two and get on with it. Looks to me like that Sammy of yours is one fine woman. You'd better hang on to her."

"I wish it were that simple."

"Simple? Not much of life is simple, my friend. Surely you've learned that by now." Jake stepped onto a treadmill and flipped the switch. "But some things are worth fighting for. Why don't you just suck up that pride of yours and patch things up? I can't think of a single thing, short of her cheating on you, that would be worth losing her for." Jake's brow furrowed into a frown. "She didn't cheat on you, did she?"

Ted shook his head. "No, nothing like that."

"You cheat on her?"

"No!"

"I rest my case." Jake gestured toward the door. "You're wasting time, my friend. A good woman is hard to find."

Ted watched as Jake sped up the treadmill and began to jog. *Oh, Sammy, how quickly things can change. I had convinced myself I could accept the fact that those three precious children might be with you until they were grown. Then all this happened. Now what? Where do we go from here? Is there any future in store for you and me?*

æ

"You look awful," Captain Grey told Ted when he reported for work the next morning. "Don't tell me you're coming down with something. We're already shorthanded."

Ted rubbed at the back of his neck. "I'm okay. Just didn't sleep well last night."

The captain motioned toward two chairs along the wall in the day room. "I get the feeling your problem is more complicated than losing a few hours' sleep. You seem preoccupied. Wanna talk about it? I'm a good listener."

Ted moved into one of the chairs, leaned back, and locked his hands behind his head. "Because of my pigheadedness and know-it-all attitude, I've hurt the three people I love most in this world, and I don't know what to do about it."

"How about confessing you were wrong and saying you're sorry? If those people love you, surely they'll forgive you."

"Saying I'm sorry would be the same as admitting I *was* wrong."

"Were you?"

"I didn't think I was, but now I'm beginning to wonder."

Captain Grey moved to the coffeepot, poured two cups, and then handed one to Ted before seating himself. "You want to tell me what you're talking about?"

Ted stared into the cup then took a slow sip. "Sure you want hear about it?"

"Wouldn't have offered if I didn't. Does this have anything to do with Sammy?"

"Yeah. A lot to do with Sammy, but let me start at the beginning. Remember how I ranted and raved when I found out my sister had signed that donor card?"

"How could I forget?"

"For a while I guess I let my disappointment and anger about her decision consume my life."

"I'd say that fairly well sums it up."

Ted took another slow sip. "Sammy has my sister's heart."

The captain sputtered and choked on the swig of coffee he'd just taken. "What? Sammy has your sister's heart? How can that be, and why didn't you tell me about it before now?"

"I didn't know until yesterday. Neither did she."

"Man, I'm totally confused."

"If you're confused, you can imagine how I felt when I

walked into my parents' house down at Smith Springs and found Sammy sitting in their living room." Ted went on, filling the captain in on everything from the day he'd met Sammy, found out about the three children living with her, learned she'd had a heart transplant, to when he'd discovered her with his parents and that his sister's heart was keeping her alive. "I'm afraid I behaved pretty badly and said a few things I now regret. I doubt she'll ever forgive me."

Captain Grey thoughtfully rubbed at his chin. "Let's do some evaluating here, but first, let me ask you a question. Do you love Sammy?"

"I thought so."

"All I want is a simple yes or no."

Ted gazed at the ceiling, searching his heart. "Yes."

"*If* Sammy hadn't needed a heart transplant to live, would you want to marry her, spend the rest of your life with her as your wife?"

"But she—"

"Only yes or no, Ted."

"Yes, of course I would. She's the only woman I've ever wanted to marry."

Looking directly into his eyes, Captain Grey placed his hand on Ted's wrist. "Then what's the problem? You're both Christians. You both love the Lord. From my vantage point, I'd say you're one lucky man. Think about it, Ted. If it weren't for the accident, you may have never met Sammy. If your considerate sister hadn't signed that donor card, the heart you've been so concerned about, the heart that has caused a rift between you and your parents and you and the woman you love—that heart would have been buried with your sister. Is that what you wanted? Is it that hard for you to accept the fact that Sammy's life is the result of your sister's unselfish gift?"

Captain Grey's words hit Ted as hard as if he'd whopped him with a sledgehammer, and they hurt. For the first time, he could see himself for what he really was. Stubborn, selfish, and arrogant. He'd wanted things his way, not God's, and without even considering the validity of the opinions of the other people who loved his sister as much as he did.

"Each time you look at Sammy, you should feel happy and grateful to God. Only He could have caused Sammy, who was living in Denver at the time, to be the recipient of a heart donated in Nashville, and then the two of you to meet on a riverboat and fall in love. Remember what Romans 8:38 says? 'All things work together for good to them that love God.' *God* took your sister. In His plan, her time had come. You could have been taken just as easily in that accident, but you weren't. He still has things planned for you that haven't been fulfilled."

Captain Grey moved his comforting hand to Ted's shoulder. "You may have been driving that day, Ted, but none of it was your fault. God was in control. You're a great guy, one of the best. Take my advice. Life's too short to dwell on the past."

The fire bell clanged out loudly, making it impossible for Ted to respond, which was fine anyway. He needed time to mull over Captain Grey's words.

The fire was a big one—a three-story apartment building in an old, run-down part of Nashville. "Looks like they're trapped!" Cal pointed to a window on the upper floor where a woman with a baby in her arms and several small children stood waving and screaming at them.

"These old apartment buildings are nothing but tinder boxes. I'm surprised they haven't been condemned." Jake shook his head as the men quickly began to pull the heavy fire hoses from the truck and attach them to the fireplug near the front of the building.

Ted grabbed hold of the captain's sleeve. "I'll go up after them, Captain."

Captain Grey motioned toward Jake and Cal. "Cover him." The men maneuvered the hoses into place then trained the nozzles on the rusty iron fire escapes on the outside of the blazing building. "Don't take any chances, Benay," the captain called out as Ted began his ascent. "You know the rules."

Ted moved carefully up the iron rungs. Though it was difficult with all the gear strapped to him, he finally reached the third floor. "Can you make it to the fire escape?" he yelled to the woman, trying to make his voice heard above the roar.

She leaned out the window, her face contorted with sheer terror. "No! I can't carry all three of them and the baby, too!"

"I'll have to go in, Captain!" Ted was relieved when his captain waved him on. After a quick prayer for protection, he crawled through the window above the landing and, crouching, carefully made his way through the thick wall of smoke in the hall.

"Help! We're here!" he heard the woman cry as she and the children, coughing and gasping for air, moved out into the hallway. "Help us! Please help us. We don't want to die!"

Ted took the baby from her arms then grabbed hold of the oldest child's hand. "I'll take him. You hold onto my jacket and bring the others with you. Don't let go!" The woman did as she was told, and soon they were through the window and out onto the fire escape landing, near where the ladder from the truck had been moved into position.

"We need to get out of here as quickly as we can. You and

the children let the firemen help you onto the ladder. I'll take the baby down the fire escape." To his relief the woman, though panicked, shoved the children toward the ladder. As one of the firemen helped the four, Ted, with the baby held safely in his arms, carefully climbed down the fire escape to where the paramedics were waiting to check them over and assist in any way they could.

Ted smiled through his mask, then placed the baby in the mother's waiting arms. "You and the children are safe now—that's all that matters."

The woman began to weep hysterically. "We would have died up there if you hadn't come up after us. Thank you—thank you so much."

Ted smiled at her through his face mask. "All in a day's work, ma'am. Just glad to have been of service."

Captain Grey pulled him aside. "That's everyone, Ted. Good job."

"Thanks, Captain. I'd better go help Cal. Looks like that hose is about to get the better of him."

It was nearly four hours before they returned to the firehouse and another hour before the truck was cleaned and back to its shiny self. They made a few routine calls to a couple of the homes in their district and extinguished the fires quickly. Otherwise, they had no other major catastrophes the rest of the day, for which Ted was thankful. After what the captain had said to him, he had plenty of thinking to do.

As he headed for his bunk a little after ten that night, Captain Grey pulled him aside. "Come on in my office." He sat down behind his desk and smiled. "I've been thinking a lot about your situation, Ted. I saw the way you responded when you thought that woman and the children were in jeopardy. You didn't know those people. You'd never seen them before; yet you were concerned enough about them to go into that burning building without hesitation. Yes, you were covered with protective gear, and, yes, you had been trained and knew what to do. But, as you and I both know, fire of any kind is an unpredictable monster and can turn on us at any time. Explosions happen, roofs collapse, walls crumble—but did that stop you from wanting to help them? To save their lives?"

"But, sir," Ted countered, "what I did was routine."

"That may be true, but even so the element of danger was there—and you faced it head-on, without the slightest pause. Which makes me think about your sister. Didn't she do the same thing? Have a concern for those she didn't know who might be in trouble and need a heart, even though it meant going against the wishes of the brother she loved and hated to upset? I'm sure your mother would prefer you be anything but a fireman; yet you go against her wishes every time you report for work because you care." He grinned. "It sure isn't because of the fantastic money you make."

Ted nodded. "That's true. I could pull in a much better paycheck working at construction or selling used cars, though I doubt I'd be much of a salesman."

"What I'm trying to say, Ted, is that we each have to do what we have to do. Your sister did what she wanted to do by donating her heart. Sammy did what she had to do by going through the agony of the surgery and the many months of recuperation that followed. She's caring for her sister's three children because that's what she wants and needs to do. And you? You have to do what you have to do—*if* you want the woman you love to be your wife. The choice is up to you.

Don't blow it. You're a Christian. Pray about it. Seek God's will for your life."

Ted leaned toward the captain's desk and rested his elbows on its surface. "What you say makes a lot of sense."

"I'm only saying these things because I respect you. You know, Ted, God is a God of miracles. He could have come down from that cross and struck His enemies dead with a swoop of His hand, but He didn't. And He could have kept your sister alive, but He didn't. He could have kept Sammy's rheumatic fever from damaging her heart, but He didn't. But He did perform a miracle by bringing the two of you together. We don't know His will for our lives, and we certainly don't understand why He allows things to happen the way they do. But we do know this—God is in control, and we must trust Him. We have to make sure our hearts are right with Him at all times. Times both good *and* bad."

Captain Grey slowly moved his hand across the desk and cupped it over Ted's. "Just make sure your heart is right with God. If it is, all the other things will fall into place."

"Thanks, Captain. I value your counsel. As usual, you've given me a lot to think about."

Though his body was weary, Ted's mind was restless as he lay in his bunk that night and thought over the things the captain had said, especially the part about his heart being right. *Who am I kidding? My heart hasn't been right since Tiger's death. It was easy to walk with God when everything was going right, but things changed the day I lost my sister. My faith was shaken. Now, looking back, it all seems so foolish. Tiger's heart was hers to do with as she pleased. I had no right to object, and I certainly had no right to turn on Mom and Dad for supporting her decision.*

He dabbed at his eyes with the hem of the pillowcase. *How I must have grieved their hearts. How I must have grieved God's heart! And look what I did to Sammy.*

His insides ached with sorrow and regret for his thoughtless actions and words. He threw back the covers and fell to his knees beside his bunk, pouring out his heart to God, pleading for His forgiveness.

～

Sammy struggled to pull on her pajamas. Never had she been so miserable. She'd found the man of her dreams, only to lose him almost as quickly as she'd found him. "Why?" she called out to God from the depths of her heart. "Why did this heart have to be Ted's sister's? I don't mean to sound ungrateful, Father, for this extended life You have given me. But of all the hearts donated each year in the United States, why couldn't it have been someone else's?"

When the phone rang near midnight, Sammy sleepily snatched it up. It wasn't likely Ted, and she wasn't in the mood to talk to anyone else, but she didn't want it to awaken the children. "Hello."

"Hi, sis! It's me. Tawanda. Guess what? I'm going to Alaska. Did you know that in Alaska you can—"

Suddenly wide awake, Sammy sat straight up in bed. "Tawanda, where have you been? We haven't heard from you since we got that last postcard. Aren't you even interested enough in your precious children to ask about them?"

"Oh, I knew they'd be fine with you. I have to tell you where I've been. I've been to Denver, Las Vegas, Santa Fe, San Antonio, Houston, Miami, Atlanta, Chattanooga, Philadelphia—"

Sammy bit back the words she'd like to say. "When are you

coming home, Tawanda? As much as I love these adorable children, you're their mother. They need you. You can't just keep disappearing like this. You know, with my physical condition, there's a good possibility I may not be around 'til they grow up."

"Oh, don't be silly. I'll bet you're the picture of health. You should see the new motorcycle we bought with the money he won in Las Vegas. It rides like a dream. We're headed toward—"

"I don't care about your motorcycle or your boyfriend. What I want to know is when you're coming back. Your wonderful children ask about you every day."

There was a pause on the other end. "I'm not coming back, Sammy. I've never told my boyfriend I have children. If he knew, he'd leave me."

"You're not coming back? *Ever?*" Sammy wished she could go right through that phone line and strangle her sister for not caring about her children.

"No. We're getting married when we get to Anchorage. That's what I was trying to tell you. If you live in Alaska for two years, you get to share in the money the state takes in on the sale of their oil. With that and what the two of us can make picking up part-time jobs here and there, we'll be able to stay there. I know it sounds callous of me when I say it, but you can have my kids. They're yours. They probably love you more than they do me anyway, and you already have their guardianship papers."

Sammy gasped for air. "I can *have* the kids? Just like that? Like they're an old pair of shoes you've tired of? As much as I'd like it if I were their mother, I'm not. You are! You have to come back, Tawanda. *Now!*"

"You know what a free spirit I am. I wasn't cut out for motherhood."

"You should have thought of that before you had those adorable babies."

"I always thought I was being careful. I guess I wasn't, but that's okay. I'm sure they're happy staying with you. When I get a job, I'll try to send you a little money now and then to help with their expenses, but don't count on it. I've heard it's pretty expensive living in Alaska."

Sammy shook her head in bewilderment. "Have you no shame, Tawanda? To leave the precious children God gave you to run around the country with some guy you met in a bar?"

"God didn't give them to me. Those three no-good men did. Got me pregnant then deserted me—that's what they did. If I could find them, I'd give them a piece of my mind."

"Isn't that exactly what *you're* doing? Running off and deserting them? What am I supposed to tell your children, Tawanda? That their mother didn't want them? That she gave them away because they didn't fit into her vagabond lifestyle?"

"Tell them *you're* their mother now. I'm sure they'll be pleased. Especially Simon. That boy never liked me."

"It wasn't *you* he didn't like, Tawanda. It was the constant trail of men who traipsed through your house. He was filled with rage when you left like you did. He's just now beginning to get over it."

"See? What'd I say? They're better off with you. Have your lawyer draw up the adoption papers. When my sweetie and I get settled in Alaska, I'll call you with my new address, and you can send me the papers to sign."

Sammy grabbed hold of the table for support. She was so upset by her sister's uncaring attitude, she was weak. "What about Mom and Dad? Aren't you going to ask about them? Dad's health is getting worse by the week."

"Mom'll take good care of him. Tell them I said hi."

"What if something happens to Dad? How can we reach you to let you know? Do you have a cell phone?" She could almost see Tawanda's shrug of indifference on the other end of the line.

"Nope, don't have one. Maybe I'll call you when we get to Alaska. Gotta go. My honey has our motorcycle all gassed up and ready to roll. 'Bye."

A *click* sounded in Sammy's ear.

Tawanda had hung up the phone.

Sammy quietly pushed the door open to the bedroom and stood staring at the sweet, innocent faces of the three sleeping children. She hoped they hadn't been awakened by the ringing of the phone and heard her side of the conversation with their mother. "Looks like we're a family, kids. Your mom doesn't want you," she said in the faintest of whispers.

Simon lifted his head and opened one eye. "Did you say something, Aunt Sammy?"

She stepped to his bed, leaned over him and kissed his cheek. "Just that I love you, precious. Go back to sleep."

As she crawled back into bed, Sammy lifted her eyes heavenward. "Is this why You spared my life, God? So I could raise these three special children and teach them to love You? You know I'll do my best. I already love them as if they were my own. Please let me live long enough to see them through high school and out on their own before You take me. I feel humbled, yet so unworthy of being their mother. I'll never be able to do it alone. I need Your help."

Her heart filled with both joy and sadness, Sammy cried

herself to sleep, only to dream about Ted and the unpleasant way they had parted at his parents' house.

❧

She'd barely reached her office the next morning when Ted rushed in the door, sweeping her up in his arms and kissing her to the hoots and hollers of all those in the office area.

"What was that for?" she was finally able to say when he quit kissing her long enough to gaze into her eyes.

"I love you, Sammy Samuels, and I want the world to know it."

Confused, she pushed back and stared at him. "I thought you and I were through."

He wrapped his arms about her so tightly she had to gasp for air. "That was before I saw myself for what I was and begged God for His forgiveness. I was wrong, Sammy. So wrong. Can you ever forgive me?"

She glanced nervously about the room and found dozens of people staring at them. "We can't talk about this here, not with an audience."

"How about lunch?"

"I can't. Our annual employee luncheon is today. I have to be here. Can you come by my apartment tonight? About six?"

"You bet I can." Ted kissed her cheek then released her and headed for the elevator.

She watched until the doors closed behind him then, trying to maintain some composure, turned with a grin of embarrassment to the crowd of onlookers who had assembled and gave them a dismissive wave. "Show's over, folks. You can go back to work now."

Though she tried to appear calm on the outside, inside her heart was racing wildly. *Did Ted actually say he loved me?*

And asked for forgiveness? If only we could have talked, just the two of us, but not with everyone standing around gawking at us, listening to our every word. She glanced at her watch. *Nearly ten hours before I see him again? I'll never make it!*

By the time Ted arrived, she had a nice supper waiting for him, with the table set for two and candles lit. "Where are the kids?" he asked, his gaze scanning her apartment. "I brought them a new video."

"Mom came by after them. I thought it would make it easier to talk." A ripple of joy ran down Sammy's spine as Ted moved toward her, pulled her into his arms, and kissed her with a long lingering kiss. She'd thought of this moment all day, and it was as delicious as she'd imagined.

"I meant what I said this morning, Sammy. I love you," he whispered softly as their lips parted. "And I'm begging for your forgiveness. I was such an arrogant fool, thinking everyone was out of step but me. Now, thanks to God and Captain Grey, I realize I was the one who was out of step."

Sammy frowned. "Captain Grey? I don't understand."

"We had an apartment fire yesterday. A bad one. A woman and her four children could have easily lost their lives, but we were able to get them out in time."

"We? You were involved in their rescue?"

"Yeah, sorta."

By the way he dipped his head, as if wanting to avoid any praise, she was sure he had been an important part of it.

"After we got back to the station and the trucks had been washed and parked inside, Captain Grey invited me into his office, and we had a talk. He was pretty direct. He pointed out my pious attitude and other things in my life that I'd been too blind to see. Oh, I was upset with him at first, but

I respect him, not only as an honorable man but also as a Christian. I knew he was only saying those things for my good. A lot of what he said was what you, my parents, and others had been saying, but for the first time I saw myself for what I really was. Stubborn, selfish, and vindictive, and that's just the beginning of the list."

"But—"

"As I listened to his words, God spoke to my heart, reminding me of something your pastor said in his message the day I went to church with you. I remember each word as clearly as if he'd said them only moments ago. 'God's children should never put a question mark where God has placed a period.' I've tried so many times to forget those words, but I couldn't. Those words really convicted me."

He took Sammy's hand, lovingly cradling it in his own. "Although I didn't want my sister's heart taken from her, that decision was hers, not mine. And the worst part was that I was upset with God for taking my sister from me. It's a wonder you, my parents, and God want anything to do with me. What a knucklehead I've been. God has forgiven me. Now, sweetheart, I'm begging for your forgiveness."

Sammy felt like pinching herself to see if this was a dream. "Of course I can forgive you. I—I love you." Tears welled up in her eyes. "I'm glad you're no longer upset with your sister's decision, but—"

"How do I feel about Tiger's heart being your heart?"

She nodded, fearing what his answer might be.

"I've given that much thought. I'm ashamed to admit it, but I think I said something to you like, 'I hope I never meet the person who has my sister's heart.' I am so sorry for those words, sweetheart. I no longer feel that way. Knowing my sister's heart is *your* heart makes our relationship that much more special." He lifted her hand to his mouth and kissed her fingertips. "I know I don't deserve it after the way I behaved, but, please, Sammy, know that my heart is right, and I'll never say anything like that again. I promise you."

Her heart nearly exploding with love for this man, Sammy gazed up at him through misty lashes. "You have no idea how happy your words make me. I've longed for this moment—"

Ted put his finger to her lips. "Then say you'll marry me, Sammy. I want you to be my wife. I want us to be together forever."

Sammy stared at him. "Did you say m—m—marry you?"

Scooping her up in his arms, he whirled her about the room. "Yes, I said marry me! I love you, sweetheart. You mean everything to me. We belong together."

Suddenly her sister's phone call came to mind, and she pulled away from his grasp, her newfound joy turning into a terrible ache in the pit of her stomach. "I can't—we can't do this. I love you with all my heart, Ted, but—"

He reached for her hand, his questioning eyes fixed on hers. "But why? We both love each other, and you said you'd forgive me."

Sammy swallowed at a lump in her throat that threatened to choke her. "My sister called. She's not coming back for the children."

"Not coming back now?"

"Not ever. She gave them to me."

"Gave them to you? Permanently?"

Sammy nodded. "She told me to have a lawyer draw up the adoption papers." As much as she loved Ted, she loved the children, too. They were, and would continue to be, her first priority. They had to be. "Tawanda had no interest in them at all. She didn't even ask about them. It broke my heart. Those children need their mother."

Ted wrapped her tightly in his arms again. "They don't need her, sweetheart. They need you. The love you have for them and the care you give them are far more than their mother ever gave them. I'd say God gave them to you for that very reason."

"But that means they'll always—"

"Always be with you?"

"Yes, as long as God gives me breath."

He tilted her face up to meet his. "And you think I might not want to marry you because of them?"

"Yes," she answered in a mere whisper.

"You're worrying needlessly, dearest. True, I haven't spent a great deal of time around the children, but I've seen the look of excitement in Simon's eyes when we play catch. That boy needs a father figure in his life. I'd like to be that father figure. And Tina? What a joy that little girl is. Her smile and her sweet gentle ways are so like yours. She even looks like you." He gestured toward a photograph on the end table. "And little Harley? Who wouldn't love that precious child, with her cute little button nose and those big blue innocent eyes? I've grown to love those children, Sammy. I'd be proud to become their uncle and help you with them. I'm sure at times it'll be hard, but doesn't anything worthwhile take time and effort?"

Sammy savored his words, words she'd never expected to hear when she'd told him about Tawanda's call. But she was still filled with uncertainties. Did Ted have a realistic idea of what he might be getting into? From being a confirmed bachelor to becoming a husband and sharing the raising of three children was a considerable leap. "Are you sure you mean that, Ted? Living with three children isn't easy. You've already complained about living with your nephews. Maybe you'd better give this considerable thought before committing yourself to what could be a long-term task."

Smiling at her, Ted brushed an errant lock of hair from her forehead. "I've already thought about it. I've spent quite a bit of time with my brother and his family lately, and you know what? I've actually enjoyed being around them. The children are a little rough around the edges, but they're pretty good kids. I'm getting along well with my sister-in-law now, and my brother and I are closer than we've ever been."

"Oh, Ted, I'm glad for all of you."

"Me, too. Now all I need is for you to say you'll marry me." Reaching into his pocket, he pulled out a small gold ring. "I was hoping you'd forgive me, so I stopped by the jewelers this afternoon. I'm waiting, dearest. What's your answer?"

How she longed to let Ted slip that ring onto her finger as a symbol of their love and commitment, but she couldn't. "You need to consider something else," she confessed with a heavy heart, her hand touching the neckline of her blouse. "Your sister's heart has given me new life, but there is no assurance how long that life will last. I may have one more year, maybe five, maybe ten. As a heart transplant recipient, my life span isn't as long as most folks' might be, and there's always the chance of complications. You've already lost your sister. Do you want to take a chance on marrying someone who may not have many years of life left? Who takes medication every day of her life? Who constantly has to go to the doctor for checkups?"

Ted gazed into her eyes with love. "According to the law of averages, Tiger, who was in excellent health, should have lived at least into her seventies, but she didn't. Her life was taken in that accident. None of us knows how long we're going to live. Only God knows. Whatever time either of us may have, my darling, I want us to spend it together. So—my answer is yes, I *do* want to marry you, knowing all those things."

His words made her heart soar with anticipation, but she knew she had to bring up one other thing. She paused then reached up to her neckline, unfastened the top two buttons of her blouse and spread the collar tabs open wide. "Though you've only seen the tip of this unsightly scar, it runs all the way to my waist. I'm not the beautiful unblemished wife you deserve, Ted. Are you sure you want to live with a woman disfigured like this? See this jagged, ugly scar every day? Be reminded of your sister's thoughtful act?"

Ted studied the scar for a moment then bent and kissed the indentation area slightly above her collarbone, the area where the scar began. "Your scar isn't ugly, sweetheart. It's beautiful. Beautiful because it gave you life. I won't mind seeing it and touching it. In fact, I'll consider it an honor because, without it, there would be no you, the woman I love." Tenderly he kissed the scar again. "Will you marry me, Sammy, be my wife?"

Her hand flew to cover her mouth as an overwhelming love rushed to the surface and spilled down her cheeks in the form of tears. Unable to speak, she simply bobbed her head.

Ted let loose an enthusiastic laugh. "I take it that's a yes?"

She threw her arms about his neck. "Yes, it's a yes! Oh, Ted, I can't tell you how much I love you. Words can't express how happy you've made me."

Taking her hand in his, he gazed into her eyes. "Sammy Benay. I like the sound of that. Or how about Rosalinda

Benay? That has a nice ring to it. Hmm, Mrs. Ted Benay. I like that even better. Now are you going to let me put this ring on your finger or not?"

"Yes, oh, yes, Ted. I'd love to wear your ring." Sammy couldn't help but stare at the ring as he slipped it onto her hand. It was the most beautiful ring she'd ever seen. "I love it. This ring is precious because it symbolizes the life we plan to have together. I'll treasure it always." She leaned into him reveling in the warmth and strength of his embrace as Ted circled his arms around her and pulled her close.

"So when should we get married?"

"When?" Lifting her face to his, she gazed into his clear blue eyes, delighting in the love she saw reflected there. "I don't know. Don't you want time to get better acquainted with the children first? Make sure you'll be comfortable living with them?"

"I don't need time, Sammy. I love those kids and have already wasted too many years of my life. I'd like us to get married as soon as possible. Of course we'll have to find a house first. I don't think your apartment could hold one more person, and I told my brother he and his family can stay at my place for as long as they need."

Her eyes widened. "You have?"

"Yep."

"So we're going to look for a real house? Not an apartment?"

"Yes, a real house. One big enough for the five of us and any children we'll be adding to our family."

Her jaw dropped. "*Adding* to our family?"

"Sure. Even though we love your sister's children, we'll want children of our own, won't we?"

"I've always wanted children, but I wasn't sure you would.

Especially after adopting Tawanda's children."

"I want kids, too, Sammy. Our kids—yours and mine."

Both Sammy and Ted turned as the outside door opened and Simon came bursting in, throwing his arms around Ted's waist. "Did you come to play catch with me?"

Releasing his hold on his bride-to-be, Ted slipped his arm around Simon's shoulders. "Sure did, buddy. From now on, you and I are going to be playing a lot of catch."

Mrs. Samuel and the other two children appeared in the doorway. Little Harley took one look at Ted then raced across the room and leaped into his waiting arms. "Will you read me a story?"

"Sure, honey, as soon as Simon and I play a little catch." Ted reached out his free hand to Tina. "Would you like to hear Uncle Ted read a story, too?"

The little girl gave him a wide grin. "Yes, I like your stories."

Their grandmother frowned then walked over to stand by Sammy. "Uncle Ted? What's going on? Did I miss something?"

Sammy felt herself beam. "Only the happiest moment of my life. Ted and I are going to be married."

Taking on a guarded smile, her mother leaned even closer. "He knows everything?"

Sammy let out a sigh of contentment. "Everything and more. I'll tell you all about it later."

epilogue

Three months later

Ted took his place at the front of the church. From the looks of those seated in the pews, nearly everyone he and Sammy had invited had turned out for their wedding.

"You're a lucky man, Benay," Captain Grey said as he walked up and shook hands with Ted. "That Sammy is one great woman, a real gift from God. Good thing you got your head on straight before you lost her."

"I know. I was a real jerk." Ted touched his bow tie and smiled at Captain Grey. "Thanks for your wise counsel."

"I only pointed out a few things I'm sure you knew already. You just needed a little reminder."

"There's someone I'd like you to meet." Ted gestured toward the man standing on his other side. "Captain Grey, this is my best man, my brother, Albert."

The captain reached out and gave Albert's hand a hearty shake. "Nice to meet you, Albert." Then, glancing around, he backed away. "Guess I'd better find my seat. Looks as if your wedding is about to begin."

Albert leaned toward Ted. "We look pretty handsome in these black tuxedos, don't we? You're not nervous, are you?"

Ted held out his hand. "Me? Nervous? Naw, my hand always shakes like this."

Albert's face took on a somber expression. "Thanks to you and your willingness to attend that twelve-step program with me, things are going much better now. The marriage counseling Pastor Day is giving Wilma and me has helped, too. Our relationship is improving every day. Even the kids are settling down. I owe you a lot."

"You owe me nothing. I'm not a drinker, but I probably got as much out of that twelve-step program as you did. I see a lot of things more clearly now."

"I hope I'll have a job soon and we'll be out of your apartment."

"Don't worry about it. Now that Sammy and I have purchased a home, I won't be needing it. You're welcome to it."

"Wow! Thanks, Ted."

Ted glanced around the room. "I wish Tiger could have been here. I know she and Sammy would have been the best of friends, and Tiger would have loved being around the children."

Albert nodded. "I wish she were here, too. Our sister was one in a million. You suppose she's looking down at you? Watching your wedding?"

Ted grinned. "I know she is."

The two men turned their attention to the double doors at the back as the sound of the big organ filled the sanctuary. Within seconds the doors parted, and Sammy's mother emerged, followed by Ted's parents, all escorted by Ted's fireman buddies who had eagerly agreed to be ushers.

Next came two of the cutest little girls Ted had ever seen. His heart swelled with pride as Tina and Harley, in their long white dresses, slowly walked up the aisle toward him, dropping rose petals from the baskets they were carrying. Next was Simon with the ring pillow, looking quite dashing for a nine-year-old in his black tuxedo, his hair slicked down with the goop Ted had generously applied.

Ted waited anxiously as several bridesmaids came up the aisle, followed by Sammy's next-door neighbor and babysitter whom she had asked to be her maid of honor. "Sammy has to be next," he whispered to Albert, his nervousness rising to the surface.

He'd barely gotten the words out when Sammy appeared beside her father. Ted had never seen a lovelier sight. He didn't know much about fashion and what women looked for in a wedding gown, but he did know she looked like an angel in that full, filmy white dress as she floated up the aisle toward him. Her hair was tucked up under a circle-like piece covered with flowers and some kind of net attached. She looked beautiful, and the best part was—she was going to be his.

"Was she worth waiting for?"

Without taking his eyes off his bride, Ted leaned toward his best man. "You bet she was! Wow!"

When Sammy reached him, instead of waiting for her father to place Sammy's hand in his, Ted impulsively grabbed her and pulled her into his arms. He couldn't wait to hold her. So when the pastor asked, "Who gives this woman to be married to this man?" Mr. Samuel stepped forward and said, "Her mother and I."

Ted tried to keep his mind on the service, but all he could think of was the woman standing beside him who was about to become his wife. When the pastor asked each of them to recite their vows to one another, instead of saying the vows he'd rehearsed, Ted spoke directly from his heart. He ended by saying, "I promise to cherish you always, my love. I know God led the two of us together, and I praise Him for it. As for me and my house, we *will* serve the Lord. With God as my witness, I vow to do all I can to be the husband you deserve and the man you can trust with your very life. I love you, Sammy."

The pastor nodded toward Sammy. "Now, Rosalinda, you may say your vows to Ted."

Ted was sure he was the happiest man alive as Sammy gazed into his eyes and began to say her vows. He hung onto her every word, completely amazed that this moment had finally arrived after the trials and troubles they'd been through.

"I, too, promise to be the mate you deserve," she said in closing. "My heart—your sister's heart—is filled with love for you, my dearest. It is my desire that every beat of it will bring us closer together. Never doubt my love, sweetheart. I give it all to you."

Pastor Day reached out and placed his right hand on Sammy's shoulder, his left on Ted's. "Your family and friends have gathered together today to support you and help celebrate your union. May God have His hand on your marriage and may you remember the vows you have made before Him. By the power vested in me by the state of Tennessee, I now pronounce you husband and wife. Ted, you may kiss your bride."

Ted gazed into Sammy's adoring eyes as he lifted her veil. Beginning this day, he would do all he could to protect her and shield her from any harm that might come to her or threaten her life. They were a team now, and together, with God as the head of their home, they were unbeatable. He drew her close and placed his lips on hers, tasting their sweetness and enjoying the scent of her perfume.

When they parted, Sammy gazed into his eyes. Then, lifting her face heavenward, she said, "Thank You, Lord, for being patient with me and giving me this wonderful caring man."

"And thank You that my sister signed that donor card." Ted also looked upward before smiling at his beloved.

Then, hand in hand, they made their way down the aisle past family, friends, and loved ones, eager to begin the life God had given them, thanks to his sister's thoughtfulness and Sammy's secondhand heart.

A Letter To Our Readers

Dear Reader:

In order that we might better contribute to your reading enjoyment, we would appreciate your taking a few minutes to respond to the following questions. We welcome your comments and read each form and letter we receive. When completed, please return to the following:

Fiction Editor
Heartsong Presents
PO Box 719
Uhrichsville, Ohio 44683

1. Did you enjoy reading *Secondhand Heart* by Joyce Livingston?
   ❏ Very much! I would like to see more books by this author!
   ❏ Moderately. I would have enjoyed it more if

   _____

   _____

   _____

2. Are you a member of **Heartsong Presents**?   ❏ Yes   ❏ No
   If no, where did you purchase this book? _____

   _____

3. How would you rate, on a scale from 1 (poor) to 5 (superior), the cover design? _____

4. On a scale from 1 (poor) to 10 (superior), please rate the following elements.

   _____ Heroine   _____ Plot
   _____ Hero   _____ Inspirational theme
   _____ Setting   _____ Secondary characters

5. These characters were special because? _____

_____

_____

6. How has this book inspired your life? _____

_____

_____

7. What settings would you like to see covered in future
   Heartsong Presents books? _____

_____

_____

8. What are some inspirational themes you would like to see
   treated in future books? _____

_____

_____

9. Would you be interested in reading other **Heartsong
   Presents** titles? ❏ Yes ❏ No

10. Please check your age range:
    ❏ Under 18   ❏ 18-24
    ❏ 25-34   ❏ 35-45
    ❏ 46-55   ❏ Over 55

Name _____

Occupation _____

Address _____

City, State, Zip _____

SAN DIEGO

4 stories in 1

This collection unveils love's journey for four modern couples who discover that love dances through their lives when they least expect it and stays only when they are willing to hold on tight regardless of the bumps along the way. Romance at its best by authors Cathy Marie Hake and Joyce Livingston.

Contemporary, paperback, 464 pages, 5³⁄₁₆" x 8"

Hearts♥ng

HEARTSONG PRESENTS TITLES AVAILABLE NOW:

___HP449 *An Ostrich a Day*, N. J. Farrier
___HP450 *Love in Pursuit*, D. Mills
___HP454 *Grace in Action*, K. Billerbeck
___HP458 *The Candy Cane Calaboose*, J. Spaeth
___HP461 *Pride and Pumpernickel*, A. Ford
___HP462 *Secrets Within*, G. G. Martin
___HP465 *Talking for Two*, W. E. Brunstetter
___HP466 *Risa's Rainbow*, A. Boeshaar
___HP469 *Beacon of Truth*, P. Griffin
___HP470 *Carolina Pride*, T. Fowler
___HP473 *The Wedding's On*, G. Sattler
___HP474 *You Can't Buy Love*, K. Y'Barbo
___HP477 *Extreme Grace*, T. Davis
___HP478 *Plain and Fancy*, W. E. Brunstetter
___HP481 *Unexpected Delivery*, C. M. Hake
___HP482 *Hand Quilted with Love*, J. Livingston
___HP485 *Ring of Hope*, B. L. Etchison
___HP486 *The Hope Chest*, W. E. Brunstetter
___HP489 *Over Her Head*, G. G. Martin
___HP490 *A Class of Her Own*, J. Thompson
___HP493 *Her Home or Her Heart*, K. Elaine
___HP494 *Mended Wheels*, A. Bell & J. Sagal
___HP497 *Flames of Deceit*, R. Dow & A. Snaden
___HP498 *Charade*, P. Humphrey
___HP501 *The Thrill of the Hunt*, T. H. Murray
___HP502 *Whole in One*, A. Ford
___HP505 *Happily Ever After*, M. Panagiotopoulos
___HP506 *Cords of Love*, L. A. Coleman
___HP509 *His Christmas Angel*, G. Sattler
___HP510 *Past the Ps Please*, Y. Lehman
___HP513 *Licorice Kisses*, D. Mills
___HP514 *Roger's Return*, M. Davis
___HP517 *The Neighborly Thing to Do*, W. E. Brunstetter
___HP518 *For a Father's Love*, J. A. Grote
___HP521 *Be My Valentine*, J. Livingston
___HP522 *Angel's Roost*, J. Spaeth
___HP525 *Game of Pretend*, J. Odell

___HP526 *In Search of Love*, C. Lynxwiler
___HP529 *Major League Dad*, K. Y'Barbo
___HP530 *Joe's Diner*, G. Sattler
___HP533 *On a Clear Day*, Y. Lehman
___HP534 *Term of Love*, M. Pittman Crane
___HP537 *Close Enough to Perfect*, T. Fowler
___HP538 *A Storybook Finish*, L. Bliss
___HP541 *The Summer Girl*, A. Boeshaar
___HP542 *Clowning Around*, W. E. Brunstetter
___HP545 *Love Is Patient*, C. M. Hake
___HP546 *Love Is Kind*, J. Livingston
___HP549 *Patchwork and Politics*, C. Lynxwiler
___HP550 *Woodhaven Acres*, B. Etchison
___HP553 *Bay Island*, B. Loughner
___HP554 *A Donut a Day*, G. Sattler
___HP557 *If You Please*, T. Davis
___HP558 *A Fairy Tale Romance*, M. Panagiotopoulos
___HP561 *Ton's Vow*, K. Cornelius
___HP562 *Family Ties*, J. L. Barton
___HP565 *An Unbreakable Hope*, K. Billerbeck
___HP566 *The Baby Quilt*, J. Livingston
___HP569 *Ageless Love*, L. Bliss
___HP570 *Beguiling Masquerade*, C. G. Page
___HP573 *In a Land Far Far Away*, M. Panagiotopoulos
___HP574 *Lambert's Pride*, L. A. Coleman and R. Hauck
___HP577 *Anita's Fortune*, K. Cornelius
___HP578 *The Birthday Wish*, J. Livingston
___HP581 *Love Online*, K. Billerbeck
___HP582 *The Long Ride Home*, A. Boeshaar
___HP585 *Compassion's Charm*, D. Mills
___HP586 *A Single Rose*, P. Griffin
___HP589 *Changing Seasons*, C. Reece and J. Reece-Demarco
___HP590 *Secret Admirer*, G. Sattler
___HP593 *Angel Incognito*, J. Thompson
___HP594 *Out on a Limb*, G. Gaymer Martin
___HP597 *Let My Heart Go*, B. Huston
___HP598 *More Than Friends*, T. H. Murray

(If ordering from this page, please remember to include it with the order form.)

Presents

Great Inspirational Romance at a Great Price!

Heartsong Presents books are inspirational romances in contemporary and historical settings, designed to give you an enjoyable, spirit-lifting reading experience. You can choose wonderfully written titles from some of today's best authors like Andrea Boeshaar, Wanda E. Brunstetter, Yvonne Lehman, Joyce Livingston, and many others.

When ordering quantities less than twelve, above titles are $2.97 each.
Not all titles may be available at time of order.

SEND TO: **Heartsong Presents** Readers' Service
P.O. Box 721, Uhrichsville, Ohio 44683

Please send me the items checked above. I am enclosing $ _____
(please add $2.00 to cover postage per order. OH add 7% tax. NJ
add 6%). Send check or money order, no cash or C.O.D.s, please.
To place a credit card order, call 1-740-922-7280.

NAME _____

ADDRESS _____

CITY/STATE _____ ZIP _____

HP 11-06